For Ryan

Book 2

Novella Couplet

Jillian Jacobs

Published by Green Moose Productions
Copyright 2017 by Jillian Jacobs

ISBN: 978-1-942313-16-8

DEDICATION

To Jeremy.

ACKNOWLEDGMENTS

To my beta-girls.

Other Books by Jillian Jacobs

The Elementals Series

Water's Threshold

Fire's Field

Air's Vision

The O-Line Series

Ember's Center

Rachel's Guard

Maude's Score

Clayton's Star

Kindle Worlds- **Infidelity World**

Insider

Novella Duet

For April

For Ryan

CHAPTER 1

"Hello, Ryan."

Staring at her tall, beautiful form, Ryan Cole couldn't breathe, couldn't move, and couldn't force two words together. Her beautiful blue eyes and sharp jawline were highlighted with sultry makeup. Her hair was locked up tight in some sort of elaborate twist, and her skin-tight white and navy blue dress squared at her neck, revealing just enough creamy skin to make him want to rip off the damn thing.

She was here.

At his Harvard graduation reception.

With a slight smirk on those too-perfect painted pink lips.

No warning.

No text alert.

No, *Sorry, I've been absent for three years.*

Just, hello, Ryan. Well, well, wasn't April David full of surprises?

Bracing both hands on his hips, he sputtered out, "'Hello, Ryan?' You don't text to say you're coming, yet you walk in here and say 'hello, Ryan'?"

"I seem to remember someone saying if a person says hello, you're supposed to say hello back." April smirked full out now.

A hello and a smirk. *That's* what he got after waiting three long years? He knocked back the rest of his rum and coke, craving the smooth burn. Plus, maybe the alcohol would calm him enough so that he wouldn't choke her and kiss her at the same time.

"No. Nope." He held up a finger, wagging it in front of her face. "You don't get to throw *my* words back at me."

She frowned. "Are you angry? I-I'm sorry. I wanted to surprise you." She handed him a card. "Congratulations, Ryan."

Animal instincts threatened to take over. However, dropping his black dress pants and peeing in a circle around her might not be the best impression in front of his future employers—York and Graff. He'd already made sure to wear long sleeve shirts so they wouldn't see the tattoos lining his arms. And while the vision of marking his territory did ease his entirely inappropriate rage, he just took the card from her and shook his head. Of course, the minute she arrived, she had him off-kilter, yet at the same time perfectly aligned. That's what she did, had him in that zone between crazy and, well, in love.

"Listen to me, Ms. Show-up-out-of-the-blue-looking-smoking-hot-in-your-dress." Okay, did he mention crazy? Cause yeah. "We are staying here exactly one hour." Ryan stuck out his hand, waiting for her to take it. Her fear of touch might be kicking in with so many people around so reaching out would be her choice.

She smiled and gripped his hand. "All right."

Those words sealed her fate as far as he was concerned. Tied everything up in a big red bow. For now. For ten years from now. Forever.

He wrapped an arm around her waist before whispering into her left ear. "After the hour is up, I'm taking you to my place, and we're talking." Noting she had a different device in her ear, he eased back. When had that happened?

Using his forefinger, he tilted her head to the side and traced her ear's outer edge. The feel of her skin. Her rosy scent. *Fuck waiting.* "Never mind. We're leaving now."

She gripped his bicep. "Wait, I want you to meet someone."

That's when he noticed the stiff in a suit hovering behind her. An older man, maybe in his late-forties, dark hair, handsome, wearing a brown suit with a bold gold tie. He had a scholarly air, and looked as if he belonged in a Sherlock Holmes novel—as the villain.

"This is Dr. Ashburn." April waved a hand in the man's direction.

Ryan glanced at April then back to Ashburn. So this was the famous Dr. Ashburn. Her psychiatrist, therapist, or…whatever. What was the guy doing here?

Ryan held out his hand. "Nice to meet you. I'm Ryan Cole."

"Yes." Ashburn gripped his hand. "I've heard a lot about you."

Based on the I'm-going-to-fucking-smash-your-hand-to-prove-something grip, Ryan deduced Dr. Ashburn was sending a not-so-subtle message. *Got it.* Psychiatry man was warning him away. Had Ryan already lost April? Why was the doctor at her side? *Well, sorry, not sorry, Psych-boy. She's mine.*

Finished with introductions, Ryan faced April then brushed her hair behind her ear. "You never mentioned this new hearing device."

"I don't like talking about my hearing." April ducked her head. "You know this."

Ryan wasn't about to take that excuse, especially when they'd spent the last three years frequently talking about everything and anything. "I also know—"

"April." Ashburn stepped closer to April's side and took her hand. "Would you like to get something to drink?"

"Oh." She smiled at the man. "I will in a moment."

Yeah, back off. Ryan frowned and continued their conversation. "They help?" He pointed to her ear.

"To a degree, yes." She faced Ashburn then bit her lower lip as she turned back to Ryan.

Detecting her nerves, he wrapped a hand around her neck. "Dr. Ashburn, it was nice to meet you, but April and I have some catching up to do. Mainly, she's going to get an earful for surprising me like this."

Her sky-blue eyes peered into his. "Am I?"

He grinned.

She grinned back.

And for a moment the rest of the world faded away.

Ashburn cleared his throat. "April, you shouldn't leave your step-mother alone. You know how your father has a tendency to be in his own world at events like this. Cheri needs you at her side."

April spun around, searching for Cheri in the crowd before facing the therapist again. "I understand your concern, Dr. Ashburn, but I'd like to speak to Ryan. I haven't seen him in so long. If you're worried about Cheri, please go to her yourself."

"April—"

"Please, Gregory." She held up a hand, palm out. "This is what I want."

He kept her gaze for a moment then ran his fingers through his short, black hair. "All right." He patted her cheek and smiled before walking off.

Eyes narrowed, Ryan watched the guy saunter away.

April visibly took a deep breath and flashed Ryan an I'm-happy-we're-finally-alone smile. One that caused a flutter in his overly stupid and slightly desperate heart.

"Now then, perhaps we can start over." April lifted her right hand between them. "Hello, Ryan."

He shook her hand but didn't release it.

April placed her other hand on top of their joined fingers. "I have so much I want to say, but I feel...I-I think you already know."

He thought he'd known, but with the doctor skulking at her side, perhaps he'd misread the situation. *No.* He'd fought for her

5

that summer three years ago *and* during his years here. He wouldn't falter now.

Her gaze held so many questions, yet at the same time sparkled with a silent understanding that had always existed between them. "April, I'm not sure what I know, and what I don't, but I'm ready to find out." He wanted to kiss her. Wanted a physical connection and an end to this churning in his stomach. Now that she was here, he found himself a little confused on how to proceed. Sure, they'd texted and sometimes video chatted, but being together was different, wasn't it? Was she ready to love him? Was that the purpose of her visit?

He sighed and ran a hand through his recently trimmed dark blond hair. Now that she was here, they'd figure out their next steps. This sense of inner peace only existed with her, and by the smile on her face, he believed she felt the same. "Whatever it is you have to say, just know I'm happy you're here. You've made this day…perfect."

"Oh, that's very sweet. Thank you." April wiped away a tear. "I'm happy too, but Ryan, we need to talk."

Oh, those words were never good. "Sure. Let's go to—"

"Ah, here he is. The man of the hour." Indiana Senator Paul David—and April's father—smiled and slapped him on the back. "Ryan Cole. Good to see you again."

Her father's approach saved her, because one more second, and they would've been out the door and he'd have interrogated her like his very life was on the line, because it sort of was.

CHAPTER 2

Senator David flashed his politician's smile. "I see you've found April."

"Yes." Ryan nodded, squeezing April's waist. "But, I believe she found me this time."

"Good to hear. You remember, Cheri, yes? Dear, come say hello to Ryan." The senator held out an arm for his new wife.

The tall blonde gave Ryan a genuine smile as she shook his hand. "I'm very pleased to see you again, Mr. Cole."

"Thank you." The three of them together were like the poster version of the perfect family, all beautiful, blonde, and healthy. Their smiles bright white. Not a wrinkle allowed on their clothes or features.

"Congratulations on your position at York and Graff." Senator David clapped him on the shoulder this time.

April remained quiet, but Ryan felt her to the marrow of his bones. They were escaping. Soon. Reception be damned. His entire body was coiled tight and only she could offer release— both mental, and dear, God, please physical. His curiosity regarding her visit was like a bug boring into his brain, and he could only fake interest in his surroundings for so long. As it stood, he had about five seconds until his head exploded.

Yet, he prevailed for the next half hour, chitchatting with the senator while keeping April at his side. Then she and Cheri left to use the powder room. This was not at all how he'd pictured their reunion. His vision had included long kisses and a sturdy king-sized bed.

Senator David lifted his drink in a sort of mock toast. "I see you are pleased with April's visit."

"Of course I am. She's the reason I'm here today." Ryan shook his head. "Well, that and our befriend-April-agreement, for which, I'm extremely grateful."

David sipped from his whiskey glass. "Let's not dwell on past mistakes."

"April wasn't a mistake."

The senator nodded in what appeared to be agreement.

"My daughter was very concerned about how you'd feel now…after so much time apart."

"She's coming with me to Maine."

The senator bit back a smile, swirling his cubes in his glass. "I believe April has her own plans. She's become quite independent."

Ryan shoved both hands in his pockets. "I've had enough of her plans."

"I'm sure you have." Grinning, the senator met his gaze. "Thank you for being patient with her. Your time apart, though *you* may not have wished it, was good for her. I'm very proud of her progress."

Ryan wanted to ask about that progress, but he'd wait for her to tell him. He'd made the mistake of discussing April with her father before, and he wouldn't do that again.

"I imagine you two can slip out now."

"What?"

"Go. You don't need to stay here entertaining me."

"Thank you." Ryan wrapped April's father in his arms, giving him a real hug. "For everything."

"You're welcome…for everything." David patted his shoulder. "No go on. I'll smooth things over with the partners.

They *have* seen you with April, so I'm sure they'll know where you're going."

Ryan didn't know what to say to that, as this was April's father, after all. So, he nodded and made his escape.

Outside the restrooms, April and Cheri appeared, heads together, chatting.

"April."

She jumped a little. "Yes."

"You ready?"

"Ready?" She glanced at Cheri.

"To leave."

"Oh, well, actually, I meant to say…I mean, I almost forgot that I have an appointment this afternoon. Dr. Ashburn has a young lady he'd like me to meet. She's…well, Ryan, please understand…she's in a situation similar to my own. I would like to help her if I can. I told you I've been counseling young girls who've had…um…traumas…it's helped with my own recovery."

Damn it! He couldn't be resentful or jealous of her time when she had plans like that. Yet, he did wonder if the good doctor was trying to keep her occupied and away from him.

Luckily, Cheri took his hand and met his gaze before he said something not so nice about her doctor friend.

"April has fought an uphill battle for three years. She is the strongest, kindest person I know. We are staying at the Charles Hotel, and I'll make sure she sees you after her appointment." Cheri winked and dropped his hand.

Ryan nodded, grateful April had a friend to support her during the time they'd been apart. Hearing April's plans made him remember his own. "Shoot. I'm working tonight at Brown's. It's a college bar. You're both welcome to stop by. It'll be crazy."

"I'd like to attend, please." April stepped right up to him and peered into his eyes.

"Well, I'm off to find my husband." Cheri waved a hand toward the reception area. "I'll leave April with you."

"Thank you." Ryan pulled his gaze from April's and smiled at Cheri.

She nodded and left.

"I like her." Ryan faced April again.

"I do, too. You know I had a hard time trusting her at first, but we have become friends."

"I see that." After glancing around, he pulled her into a corner by an artificial ficus tree. "I understand you have an appointment, and I really want to talk about why you came. But right now, I want to hold you. Just for a moment. May I?"

"Oh, of course." April opened her arms and hugged him.

Her scent—a bouquet of freshly cut roses—drifted across his senses again. Though he hadn't been drunk in forever, he floated high on her unique April aroma. He kissed her left temple then whispered in her ear. "I've missed you so fucking much."

She eased back and clasped his face in her hands. "Ryan, I need to explain—"

"April, there you are." Dr. Ashburn stopped at her side and glanced at his phone. "We need leave in order to make our appointment on time."

"Right." April dropped her hands onto Ryan's shoulders. "Yes, of course."

Ryan didn't release her and glared at Mr. Interloper. "I can take her. We'll meet you there."

"Oh, no." Ashburn shook his head. "This party is being held in your honor. April and I couldn't ask that of you."

April and I. *Really?* This guy officially hit Ryan's last nerve. "I see." Marking his claim, Ryan leaned forward and kissed April's forehead then her cheek. "I'll text you later and save you a seat at Brown's. All right?"

"Yes."

Her word drifted like a caress against his lips, and her gaze remained locked on his mouth. *Oh honey, I'll accept that invitation.* But, if he started kissing her now, he knew the porno-police would be called, because the things he wanted to do to her mouth were filthy, naughty, and meant to make her scream.

He clenched his jaw and slowly dropped his hands from her sides.

Ashburn shifted closer and took April's arm.

"Good afternoon, Cole." Ashburn nodded then led April through the crowd.

At the exit, the dickhead glanced over his shoulder and flashed a condescending smirk.

Ryan shot him the bird, wondering what the guy would look like with the ficus tree shoved up his ass. He'd overcome a lot these past few years and so had April. Nothing and no one would keep them apart now.

CHAPTER 3

"What in the world?" April jammed the card into the hotel room door's outer lock again. "Why won't the light turn green?"

"I believe you have the card turned upside down." Dr. Ashburn stood beside her. "Here let me try."

"No." Perhaps if she had space between herself and the door, rather than trying to scoot away from the doctor who was standing far too close, she'd be able to focus on her task. She flipped the card around, slid it in quick, pulled it back out, and finally the light turned green. "Thank you, but as you can see, I fixed it myself." Head throbbing and needing a break from all the talking and thinking and just people, April slipped into her room.

Gregory held fast to the door and followed her in.

She heaved a sigh, and then slipped off her heels. "Oh, the room is lovely."

The Dean's suite had a sitting room that led into the bedroom. Everything was decorated in whites and navy blues. Blue carpet squares, distinctive New England design board-and-batten paneled walls, a blue couch, and Shaker detailed furniture. Sepia colored photos of Harvard's buildings and grounds hung on the walls.

Rubbing her feet, she turned and considered what to say to Gregory, because she didn't want to be rude, but at the same time, she could almost feel the steam pouring out her ears. If her therapist knew her so well, why couldn't he see that she was struggling? Her dress was too tight. Her stomach was grumbling, and after everything that had happened today, she needed time to reassess.

Ryan had been...well, she couldn't put the entire episode into words.

He'd wanted to drag her away, and she would have let him. Her body had melted into his arms, molding perfectly against his sturdy frame. After so many years of being afraid of another's touch, she'd broken through that phobia and now craved affection. She been dubbed the hug machine by Dewey, her sort-of bodyguard. She'd laugh and jump into his arms. Even her stepmother and father received random hugs. But when Ryan had hugged her earlier, she'd remembered all too vividly how he'd touched her intimately that summer night, far too long ago. She wanted to experience that burst of pleasure again. While understanding they were due for some serious discussions, they *could* talk in bed, between sessions of lovemaking. At twenty-four, she felt her virginity card was long overdue. She'd had many heated dreams of Ryan as a domineering librarian, stamping her card over and over again.

"April?" Dr. Ashburn stood by the desk, holding a menu in his hand and staring at her with his all-to-familiar imperious frown.

"Oh, I'm sorry." Her cheeks heated with embarrassment so she turned away and glanced out the window. "I'm distracted. Were you speaking to me?"

"Yes, I was. I imagine you're hungry. I know I am. I'll just order up something."

"That won't be necessary." April turned and took two steps toward him, fisting her hands at her sides. "I'm sorry, Dr—I mean, Gregory, but I need some time alone. Thank you for taking me to see Britni. I'll keep in touch with her as I said I would."

They'd just come from visiting a ten-year-old girl whose father had kept her captive in a basement for over two years. April understood what it meant to be trapped against her will so she'd spoken to the girl and held her as they'd both cried.

"I'd like to discuss your time with Britni." Gregory leaned against the desk. "Maybe I can help."

He had helped for a very long time. She trusted him, respected him, but nothing more. Part of her personal growth these past three years had been her realization that she needed to cope with her issues on her own without running to her therapist for answers. He was less than thrilled about this turn of events. But she couldn't let that stop her. Not with her future happiness on the line. "Oh, well, honestly, I'd like to get some rest." She turned and opened the door, hoping Ashburn would take the hint. "I plan on seeing Ryan tonight."

"I see." He nodded. "Will you at least join me for dinner?"

"No, thank you." April ran a hand over her stomach. "I'm a bit unsettled right now."

"As I mentioned before, this trip might be hard on you, which is why I feel we should discuss your feelings over dinner." He crossed both arms over his chest, tapping an index finger against his upper arm.

"That's kind of you. But I'm very tired, and I would like to take a quick nap before I go out tonight."

"April." He stepped forward and placed a hand on her shoulder. "I'll ask again that you reconsider this relationship with Mr. Cole. Please, think of your future. I can give you calm. His world is unsettled, and he can't give you the stability that I can."

April sighed and opened the door even wider. "Dr. Ashburn, I've explained that I do not have romantic feelings for you. I'm sorry to cause you pain, but I love Ryan."

"You love the idea of him."

April shook her head. "I do love the idea of him, yes. I love how I feel when I'm with him. I love his smile. His kindness. His honesty. He's very real. I need him in my life. He shakes me up."

Gregory sniffed. "April, you must prepare yourself. He might not feel the same way anymore."

"He does. I can see his feelings in his eyes." His deep-brown eyes that seemed to challenge her every time they met her gaze. A challenge she was ready to accept.

"All right, but if his intentions have altered, please come to me. We'll talk. And maybe you'll see I can be the steady beat of your heart instead of a man who, as you say, shakes it for a time." He placed a hand on her shoulder and squeezed. "You need steady and secure. I can give you that."

"Dr. Ashburn, please. I don't wish to have this discussion again. I'll see you in the morning. I'll text you, and we can have tea together, all right?"

"Yes, that'd be perfect. And, please call when you get home tonight so I don't worry."

"I will." She eased away from his touch. She'd never included her doctor in her hug-machine, as she hadn't wanted to cross any barriers, and after his recent revelation, she was happy she'd kept her distance.

He frowned, opened his mouth to speak, but then shook his head and left.

Shutting the door, April heaved a long sigh, took five steps to the bed, and collapsed. Eyes drifting closed, she tried to sleep but her mind whirled with too many thoughts.

Was Ryan still in love with her? Had they both changed too much? Had she helped Britni today? How would she get to Brown's tonight? And what should she wear?

Nothing had gone as she'd wished during their reunion. They hadn't had a chance to talk. She'd envisioned walking up to him and declaring her devotion forever. But that couldn't have happened in a crowded room. Plus, his graduation reception had been about him, and she'd been too wrapped up in her own needs to understand she should've just celebrated his accomplishments

15

instead of her own. She'd spent so much time concentrating on her personal growth, she'd become a tad self-centered. That would need to change. She would simply ask Ryan what he wanted and needed from her. People in relationships did that, right?

Groaning, she rolled onto her stomach, sat up on her elbows, and punched the pillow. "Gah! I hate this! I have no idea what I'm doing." She plopped her face into the pillow. It smelled clean enough, but she'd still spray the bed with Lysol. People did unsanitary things in hotel beds. Even in nice places like this one. Done suffocating herself, she shifted to her side and locked one arm around the pillow under her head.

She'd promised to visit Britni again tomorrow afternoon. Would Ryan go with her? She'd rather not go with Dr. Ashburn. He'd made their whole relationship awkward to the point she didn't want to spend time with him anymore. He knew too much about her, but he didn't really know the yearnings of her heart. And she'd never discussed her sexual frustrations.

Had Ryan been with other women during their time apart? He'd never mentioned other women during their chats, except for his friend, Shelby. Not that he would. She sighed. "You let him go, silly. So, you can't have any say in his…sexual choices. Still, I don't like it at all." Huffing out a breath, she fisted her hand in the plump white comforter.

A knock sounded on her door.

She rolled her eyes. Hadn't she made herself clear to Dr. Ashburn? Maybe she'd pretend to be asleep. But what if it was Ryan? Had she told him where she was staying? She couldn't remember. Not after everything that had happened today.

Shuffling over to the door, she looked in the peephole. A blurry Cheri stood on the other side. "Yes?"

"April, it's Cheri."

"I can see you." She opened the door.

Cheri stepped inside and looked around. "How is the room?"

"I like it." April slid over to the blue couch and held one of the checkered pillows in her hands. She squirmed a little. Her pantyhose needed to come off, very soon.

Cheri sat beside her, folding both hands in her lap. A body-language skill her father's public relations people had taught them. Look serene. Smile. Bend your legs to the side. Stick to discussions on weather and charity work.

"What are your dinner plans, April?"

"I believe I'll call room service."

"And your plans for later?" Cheri arched her blonde brow.

"I thought today would go differently. I had all these romantic notions." She shook her head. "I need to see Ryan alone. I have so much to say, and so does he...at least that's what he said. He wanted to leave with me, but I had to see Britni with Dr. Ashburn."

"He did that on purpose, you know."

"Who?"

"Nothing." Cheri's lips pursed. "I shouldn't involve myself."

"Please don't do that. Don't shelter me from your thoughts."

"All right." Her stepmother faced her. "While I think Dr. Ashburn introducing you to Britni was a very kind thing, I don't believe his actions were altruistic."

"I agree." Her stomach grumbled again. She really needed peppermint tea and a huge chicken sandwich or maybe pizza. Something. "No matter how many times I express my feelings, he doesn't hear me. Not really." April tugged the pins out of her hair and then rubbed her aching scalp. "I believe Dr. Ashburn wants me to fail, and I'm not sure how I feel about that, especially after he spent so many years helping me succeed. It's a very odd and uncomfortable situation."

"He needs you to need him."

"I *need* Ryan."

Cheri stood and grabbed the room service menu off the desk. "He still loves you."

17

April's head shot up and she met Cheri's blue eyes. "How do you know?"

"I just do." She shrugged.

"Well, I don't."

"Deep in your heart, you do. Now, chin up." Cheri tipped up April's chin and gave her nose a tap. "Let's find you something to wear that'll knock his socks off."

April rose from her seat and patted the top of her dress's zipper. "I thought I'd rest first, but I can't shut down my brain."

Cheri slid the zipper down halfway. "Now." She tapped her fingers against April's bare back. "Go shower and I'll get your outfit out of your suitcase and order room service. If you're tired after eating, you can rest for a while then."

"Good idea." April kept a hand pressed against the front of her dress. While she was comfortable around her stepmother, she wasn't drop-her-dress comfortable. Before stepping in the bathroom, she hugged Cheri from behind with her free arm. "How are you?"

"I'm fine." She chuckled. "Why do you ask?"

"Because I feel I don't ask enough how *you* are. You always help me, have always been very kind, and I worry I may be self-centered."

"You're young." Her shoulders lifted.

"That's not a good excuse." April eased back and pressed against Cheri's shoulder so she'd turn. "I appreciate you, Cheri. And I-I love you."

"Well, thank you." Cheri wiped a tear from her eye. "Now stop, or you'll ruin my mascara." She squeezed April's hand. "I love you, too. Well...anyway...go get cleaned up so you can wow your man."

April nodded. "He *is* my man, isn't he?"

"Based on the way Ryan looks at you, I'd say, yes."

"How does he look at me?"

"That's easy. As if he'd scale mountains, fight tigers, jump through fire, and beat back hoards of angry moose."

"Angry moose?" April bent over laughing. "Oh, Cheri, that's funny."

Cheri smiled and wrapped her in a hug. "I know. I'm a comedian, but nothing is funny about the way that man looks at you. Now go get ready before the moose attack."

April laughed all the way to the bathroom, grateful to Cheri for once again filling in for the mother she'd lost long ago. No, not lost. Her mother had chosen to leave her behind. And that truth kept an open ache in her heart. But she lived with the pain of her mother's suicide, and she'd moved forward. Now that her head and heart were straight, she'd spend more time appreciating those who had seen her through her tough times.

She was ready to scale her own mountains and, if necessary, fight off a few moose of her own.

CHAPTER 4

A bead of sweat trickled down Ryan's back, and he did a little shimmy, hoping his T-shirt would rub against the minor annoyance. Music blaring. Bodies bopping. Drinks flowing. Tonight was a helluva scene at Brown's. The semester was over and it seemed as if the entire student body had descended on this bar.

His first year at Harvard had been about discovery. Older than most of the students, he'd already sowed his oats, but adjusting to Ivy League life had been a touch interesting for an Indiana kid. Now, with his degree in hand, everything aligned except one thing—April. Yet, that situation would be remedied before he started his new job.

Waiting for April had him ramped up, but he loved the chaos, the people, and their joy at the end of all the hard work. Tonight was his last night bartending after a fun, yet sometimes crazy, three-year run. He'd actually planned on breaking his own rule and drinking tonight, but now that April was on her way, he'd sidelined that idea.

Popping the cap off a Sam Adams, he slid the bottle down the bar and grabbed the credit card from a giggling redhead.

She winked. "Want to do a shot?"

Her east-coast accent was prevalent with the emphasis on the "a's."

"I'll do a shot." A familiar voice answered. A voice that slid across his nerves and sounded a lot like home.

He spun around, grinning like an idiot.

The redhead gave April a once over. "Wasn't talking to you, sweetheart."

"Okay." After quickly swiping the card, Ryan handed it back before things got ugly. "No shots." He grinned at the redhead and pointed to the iPad's screen for her to sign. "Thank you anyway. April, sit down right here, please." He waved toward a bar stool he'd reserved for her by tying a sign to both arms. "Just untie the knot."

She did as he requested and rolled the string around the poster he'd made out of an empty cardboard beer box. Then she slid into her seat. She'd certainly improved her clothing choices. Daddy hadn't bought those skinny jeans and her green She-Hulk top that had some kind of shimmery fabric along the neckline. A low-cut neckline. A highlighting-a-gorgeous-chest neckline.

"Hi, Ryan. How are you?"

Her question came across very earnest. He bit back a smile. His woman was as polite as ever. "I'm very busy. How are you?" He could do formal if that's what she wanted. Maybe she was nervous. He sure the hell was if his pounding heart had any say in the matter.

"I am happy to be here." She blinked and leaned her left elbow on top of the bar.

Ryan blocked out all the people hollering for his attention. "How'd your meeting go?"

"What?" April held a hand up by her ear.

"Never mind. I'll ask you later."

She nodded. "Don't worry, Ryan. I'm not scared to be in a bar anymore. I don't like being shoved, but that's perfectly normal. I also don't like people spilling their drinks on me."

"No one will." Good God, she was really here. While true,

they'd spoken frequently, they'd only seen each other in person once. About a year ago, she'd arrived at his apartment in the middle of the night, eyes red and body shaking. The minute he opened the door, he jolted back as she jumped into his arms and burst into tears. He held her as she recounted her visit to Sierra Leone. The place where, as a child, she'd been held captive for almost two months. After her tears were spent, he railed at her for going to such a dangerous place. He'd never been so angry. He even called her father and Dewey to give them a piece of his mind. How stupid could they be?

She'd arrived on a Monday night, and he had a major exam on Tuesday, so they hadn't had much time together before she left. She held his hand on the way to the airport and asked him to give her time. And though their separation drove him insane, he'd let her go. Again.

Before he'd left for Harvard initially, they'd made a pact to try to connect every other Sunday. During those chats, they spoke of mundane things, rarely delving deep, but through those conversations he'd grown to love her more.

He loved her drive to improve. Her literal interpretation of practically everything. Her intelligence. Her sunny outlook even after a traumatic past. Her unwavering belief in him. And her utterly flawless beauty.

Seeing her in the flesh had his cock going from 'just chilling,' to 'I need to fuck' in an instant. *Cool it! She might not be ready.* Was she ready? Please, please let her be ready.

"I'd like to sit here and absorb the atmosphere. I won't disturb your work." April turned and studied the beer taps for a moment, brow narrowed a bit, and chewing her plump lower lip. "I haven't ever partied in a college town, so this will be interesting."

Yeah, it'd be interesting all right. He had no idea how he'd make it through the rest of the night. He grabbed a bar towel and gripped it in his hand to keep from reaching across the bar and kissing her senseless. "What do you want to drink?"

"I will have a beer."

"What?"

"Beer." She flicked a hand toward the taps. "You serve all kinds, right?"

Hell yes, he served all kinds. And he'd love to serve her. On the bar. Over the bar. Across the bar. Whatever. Whenever. Now. Later. *Fucking hell.* He bit back a groan. "I'll give you whatever you want." Customers were shouting, waving money around, but he was stuck right here. With April.

"Will you?" She smiled then licked her lower lip. "Anything I want?"

"You teasing me now?"

"I have no idea what you mean."

Well now, look who'd turned into Ms. Coquette. *Oh, yeah this flirt-fest was on.* Wait a minute…she wanted beer? Had she been frequenting bars?

"April, have you been drinking?"

"Um…no." She frowned and shook her head.

So literal. He chuckled and grabbed a clean glass. "That's not what I meant, but never mind. What would you like?"

A tall, jock-looking douche in a Harvard swim team shirt pressed up against April. "Hey man? Can I get a beer?"

Ryan held back an inner growl when the guy glanced at April then did a double-take before saying, "hey" and settling in.

April smiled at swim guy, revealing a row of perfectly white, perfectly lickable teeth. "Ryan." April faced him again and shouted over the music and general mayhem. "In answer to your question, I'll have whatever is on draft that has an orangey flavor, all right?"

"Blue Moon is *orangey*." Swim-team jock piped up and held out his hand. "I'm Cory."

No. Tonight would not go like this. Ryan practically growled, "She's April and she's with me, so take your money and move along."

"Ryan, that's rude." April gasped, and stared at him with wide eyes.

"I don't give a shit."

April shrugged and mumbled, "sorry" to Mr. Fish-face still standing beside her.

Cory smiled. "I get it, man. She's something else. What are you like a model or something?"

Oh dear, God. Lame!

April shook her head. "No. I am not a model, and I know I'm pretty, but I can't do anything about it."

Cory chuckled, obviously charmed. "Well...you could be."

"All right. Here is your beer, April. Swim-jock, go fish somewhere else."

The guy tipped his chin and left.

April sipped her beer. Her phone pinged, and she frowned after looking at the screen.

"So, you're drinking beer now?"

Her gaze stayed on her phone for a moment before she placed it face down on the bar. "I like beer sometimes. I also like red wine. Maria and I watch movies and have crackers and wine. Dewey says we're too high-society for him."

"How's the big guy doing?"

"What?" She cupped a hand up by her ear.

"Give me a minute." *Damn it.* No way could she hear overly well in this zoo. Standing on this side of the bar, he wasn't close enough. He needed to hold her again. Needed answers. He grabbed John, the other bartender, by his arm. "Hey buddy, I need five."

"Are you insane?" John waved a hand at the mass of people surrounding the bar.

"Yes."

"Three minutes."

"Four."

"Fine," John growled. "Make it quick."

Ryan scooted down the bar and lifted the pass-thru then hustled to April's side. But once he got there, he wasn't sure what to do or what to say. He could barely breathe, so he blurted out, "So." *Genius! What a way to say you care.*

She smiled and turned in her seat. "Are you finished?"

"No, I only have a few minutes."

"Oh, okay." She ran her hands up and down her thighs. "It's very busy in here tonight."

"Yeah." Okay, this was awkward. He needed shots, something that would burn all this trepidation from his throat. He tapped a finger against her glass. "When did you start drinking beer?"

"I told you I go to bars with Dewey and Maria sometimes. Then I sometimes go out with my boxing class friends." Her lovely head tilted to the side. "Remember, we talked about this before."

They had, yes. Still, what did that mean? During their time apart, he hadn't dated anyone else, but she'd never said if she had or not…and he'd never asked. He cleared his throat and ignored the glare from John. "So, did you meet anyone when you went out?" Why was this so weird? He was acting as if he didn't really know her, but he did. Where the fuck was all this self-doubt coming from? It sucked serious ass, and he wanted it gone.

"Yes." She nodded. "Men would speak to me, offer to buy me drinks, ask for my phone number. They would sometimes say I was beautiful. It's hard to hear in these places though, so I'd usually just smile, which sometimes made them angry."

Leaving caveman fury aside for a moment, he cupped her face. "April, you do realize that your looks are extraordinary, right?"

She met his gaze, her blue eyes blazing. "Ryan, you do realize that *you* are very extraordinary, right?"

"Not even close to you." He'd missed her face, sure, but he'd missed her honesty and innocence even more. He'd missed the way her eyes lit up when she saw him. Her rapt attention when he spoke. She was so much more than her outer beauty. She was his brave April.

"I don't want to talk about me anymore." April tore away her gaze and pressed her lips together before she took a sip from her beer. "People are waiting for their drinks. I don't want you to get in trouble for talking to me."

"You are trouble. Showing up here without telling me. I'm still not sure what that's all about."

"Hey, Cole." John hollered from across the bar, tapping his wrist. "Your four minutes are up."

April glanced at John then back at him. "I'm sorry. I'll just wait for you right here."

"You'll wait for me? Woman." He shook his head then kissed her. Hard. Gripping the back of her neck, he held her in place as he basically assaulted her mouth, rasping his tongue across hers until she moaned and arched toward him, practically sliding off her seat. Once neither of them could breathe, he growled into her left ear. "This waiting shit is over."

"Yes, it is." She raked her fingers through his hair. "We have a lot to discuss."

He eased back and met her gaze. "This discussion is only paused, you hearing me, April David?"

"I hear you." She tapped her ear. "Now, get back to work."

Grumbling under his breath about bossy females, he rounded the bar, and then pasted on a fake smile and served patrons who spent more time checking their phones than speaking to one another.

About an hour later, and after only a few rounds of chitchat with his woman, he glanced down the bar while preparing a round of shots for a group of sorority sisters. Tonight, he wasn't in the mood to flirt back to bulk up his tips. His attention was on a blonde in a tiny green She-Hulk top, and the amazing kiss they'd shared earlier. Fuck, he could still taste her. He fought back a shiver and spared a quick look at his infatuation once more. He'd asked one of his trusted pals to watch out for April tonight not realizing seeing them laughing while he had to tend to giggling simpletons would seriously test his patience.

Right now, Big Bane was in some animated discussion with April, his hands waving madly as he acted out something. Bane was the middle linebacker for the football team. Out of all his friends, Ryan knew Bane would keep everyone in check.

After pouring the round of shots and taking the girl's money, he headed down the bar. "April, you need anything?"

Her cheeks were rosy from the beer most likely. Although all the bodies crowding the bar kept the temperature just-past steamy.

She stretched her hand across the bar. "Can you take a break now?"

Her smile seemed a little lopsided. Funny, as she'd only had two beers.

He took her hand and kissed it. "No more beers for you. Let me get you a water." He opened the cooler and pulled a bottle from his personal stash.

"Thank you." She opened the bottle and took a long drink. "Ryan, there's something I need to—"

"We never believed him." Bane set his arm along the back of April's chair.

Ryan watched for signs that his friend's touch bothered her, but she didn't flinch. He loved the guy, but he'd interrupted whatever April had been about to say. He flicked a finger at Bane. "Yep, she's real. Very real."

"Lucky bastard." Bane gave him a middle finger salute.

Ryan grinned then faced April, a tinge of unease in his stomach. "What were you—"

"I can see why Ryan waited for you, sweetie." Bane shot a glare at a guy stepping up on April's other side. "I'm keeping an eye on her, Ry. No problem, man. Though Shelby drifted by earlier." Bane circled an index finger by his ear. "Coo-coo. That chick's not right."

That's all Ryan needed to add to the frustrations of the night. A jealous friend. He grabbed his own water bottle and took a long drink. Wiping off his mouth, he shrugged a shoulder. "Shelby knew the score."

"That one is mental with a capital M." Bane finished off his beer and handed the glass to Ryan. "One more, Ry. Same as usual."

"*Who* is mental?" April batted those thick, dark brown lashes. "Does someone like you, Ryan?"

He avoided her gaze and filled Bane's glass.

"That's an understatement," Bane mumbled.

Luckily, with all the noise, Ryan doubted April had picked up on his friend's comment. He slid Bane a full glass of beer and leaned closer to April so she could hear him. They had enough to work out without adding complicated friendships that weren't really complicated. "I have a friend named Shelby. I've mentioned her before. She's a bit…overzealous…and confused as to her role in my life. I've explained things, and I told her about you, but…" He ran a hand through his hair, the longer strands on top had lost all product hours ago, so they were flopping onto his forehead. "She's sort of in denial or whatever."

"Oh, right, I remember. You mentioned she's your study partner." April glanced over her shoulder then back at Bane. "Was she the brunette from earlier? The one with the tattoos and almost yellow eyes? Yes, she was very pretty." She slumped a little and spared Ryan a glance, her teeth digging into her bottom lip. "I thought something might be wrong since she immediately left after Bane introduced us." April fluffed her hair over her ears.

A familiar nervous habit. *There* was *his* April. Not that he wanted her to be the same. To be frightened or nervous. He *did* want her stronger than before, but he hadn't quite recognized her yet, but with that action, he relaxed a little. He didn't know if she was self-conscious about people seeing her hearing devices or what her movements represented, but her actions were pure April.

Ryan jolted out of his musings when a skinny kid with huge Hubble-Telescope glasses tapped the bar with his empty glass.

"I've got to get back to it." Ryan shot Bane a keep-her-safe glare.

Bane nodded. "April, don't worry about Shelby, okay?"

"It seems as if I should, though." Her brow furrowed and she sipped from her water bottle again, avoiding Bane's gaze.

"Hey." Ryan tapped her arm. "Don't do that. Don't worry about Shelby or anything else, all right?" He waited for April to nod. "We'll talk here in a bit. You stick by Bane, okay?"

She smiled in return but it was a weak effort. "Maybe I should go."

"Sit your ass in that chair. You don't get to just pop in and out, like some whack-a-mole game. You came to me, and we're doing this. So, sit."

April narrowed her eyes but remained seated. "I had a lot to say to you before, but now, you're really gonna get it."

He grinned and spread his arms wide. "Oh, baby. Hit me with your best shot."

She pressed her lips together, glared a little, and then turned away and began speaking to Bane.

Well now, apparently Ms. David had dismissed him. While chuckling over her actions, Ryan served the skinny kid and about a zillion others, all while keeping an eye out for Shelby. Now that April was here, something Shelby hadn't known would happen, he wondered how his friend would deal. He already knew the answer to that. Shelby would freak the fuck out. This night had the potential to go south fast. Though he'd explained over and over about April, he wondered if Shelby had ever truly believed the depths of his feelings.

While prepping a fuzzy navel, he watched as Shelby sauntered up to the bar, her eyes red and practically closed. Was she high? *Fucking hell.*

"So, I see your Barbie doll came fresh from the factory. Didn't know she was scheduled for delivery." Shelby laughed, but the sound was hollow and forced. "That…woman looks like a fake-ass beauty queen. Really, Ryan? I mean, seriously. Her?"

Then she spoke in a high-voice with some kind of accent he couldn't quite decipher.

"Hi, I'm miss Indiana. I'm a perfect senator's daughter. I have perfect blonde hair, blue eyes, and enormous tits. Where's her stupid sash, Ryan? Oh, oh, I know…it'd say, I'm a perfect cunt."

"Shelby," he growled in warning. "Don't. I didn't know April was coming today." He'd let Shelby's comments slide, because, well…April *was* kind of like a Barbie doll in the flesh, and he wanted nothing more than to play dress up—or more likely, dress off.

"Oh, yeah. Sure, you didn't." Slurring her words, Shelby wagged a black-painted fingernail in his face. "That woman down there is *so* not you. She's smells like flowers for fuck's sake. I don't know why I ever worried." She hiccuped. "Capital C. Cunt."

"Enough, Shelby." Ryan hated the c-word, but Shelby seemed to like using it to describe any woman who showed him the slightest interest. He'd given his friend a moment to express her shock over actually meeting April, but that was done now. Sure, Shelby was hurting, but insults were insults. And her words were entirely uncalled for. "Again, I didn't know April was coming. But that doesn't matter, she's here and I couldn't be happier." He met Shelby's watery gaze. "You don't know her."

"I don't have to *know* her." Shelby rolled her eyes. "I *see* her, and she's all wrong. Pffttt…wrong."

There was no arguing with her, plus she was drunk or high or both. His heart swelled with sympathy. They were friends, after all, and the one woman Shelby hadn't wanted to believe was real, was here—live and in the flesh. Yet, Shelby had no right to judge April on her looks.

She didn't know of April's struggles and triumphs. He'd never shared any part of April, or his real self with Shelby, so he couldn't fault his friend for not seeing that April *was* his perfect match. He took a deep breath and focused on wrapping up this conversation because Shelby needed to go home and sleep off whatever was in her system. "Who are you here with?"

"Why do you care?" She flashed a fake grin.

Heaving a sigh, he grabbed a water bottle out of the cooler and set it in front of her. "Drink this."

"Fuck off." She emphasized her words with her middle finger then flung her hand against the bottle.

It flew off the bar and bounced against the concrete floor.

Ryan arched a brow. Then he picked up the bottle and tossed it in the trash before moving down the bar to serve other customers. Well, that had gone about as well as expected. Jaw clenched, he flicked on the tap and filled another beer glass.

A musical sound hit his ears. April laughing. Shaking off his conflict with Shelby, he glanced down the bar.

April's head was thrown back, her smile wide, her eyes dancing. Three years ago, she'd never have done that. And for the first time, he actually felt that their time apart had been good for her. If she could laugh like that, be around a new person and express her joy, then maybe, just maybe she'd found some peace and was ready move forward.

She lightly touched Bane's arm, and that simple motion almost brought a tear to his eye.

He'd thought her beautiful before, but now that she'd finally escaped from her cage, now that she was flying free, she was the most exquisite woman he'd ever seen. Not right for him? Hell, they'd both walked through fire, and together they'd forge a future.

April looked his way and smiled.

He winked in return then got back to work.

CHAPTER 5

April stood outside the bar's bathroom door and fought to breathe. So disgusting. Maybe she should go outside and get some fresh air. Or better yet, go back to the hotel and shower the filth from her body. She shivered then pulled her tiny rose scented sanitizer from her purse and squeezed it all over her hands and arms.

When two girls walked by and gave her an odd look, she realized what she was doing. *Stop it!* Just breathe. They'd done studies on public bathrooms and found most people's hands were dirtier than anything else. *I've got this. Don't let the phobias take control. I am here for Ryan. Don't miss another moment.*

Three years, two months and five days. That's how long she'd been without him. Her triumphs over her phobias during that time had been hard-fought and some days not completely won, but that no longer mattered.

She was here to claim her reward. No more isolation, fear of germs, or fear of touch. Now, she craved that dizzy feeling brought on by Ryan's kisses. When he'd kissed her earlier, her whole body had lit up and declared, "just fall, he'll catch you."

She'd asked Ryan for time and he'd given it to her. However, lately Ryan mentioned his friend, Shelby a lot. Every time April thought of him with Shelby, she practically bent over with the acrobatics occurring in her stomach. She hadn't asked Ryan to explain the full extent of his relationship with the woman, because she didn't really have the right. Was she too late? Had he moved forward while she'd remained in the past? And what kind of person was she to believe that just because she was ready for more, he would be too?

Through ruminating, she squeezed through the mesh of bodies and two guys who were kissing...*oh my*. She inched toward her chair then halted to a stop when someone wrenched on her arm.

Frowning, she spun around. "Let me go."

"I wanna talk to you." Shelby stood at her side, her grip quite strong.

The smell of booze and something else, like burnt flowers exuded about as strong as the glaring hatred in her gaze. Her eyes were bloodshot and the tip of her nose was bright red. Maybe she'd been crying.

"What do you wish to speak about?"

"That right there!" Shelby jabbed a finger in her face. "Who talks like that?"

April sniffed, and lifted on her toes in an attempt to catch Ryan's eye. Failing at that, she studied Shelby again, unsure how to proceed as this was a foreign situation. "I don't know what you mean, but I will say, I had a different education than most so I may not be as up to date on the current slang." *Perfect, April. That whole sentence didn't just prove Shelby's point.* She sighed.

Shelby stared at her for a second then laughed hysterically, dropping her head back on her shoulders. "Oh, this is classic. You are *so* wrong for him. What a joke."

"I am not." April pulled her arm from Shelby's grip. "I know I haven't been...*here*, but we've still talked. I am *not* wrong for Ryan. I'm sorry if you're hurting. You appear to have been crying."

Shelby scoffed and shook her head. "Oh honey, *I'm* not hurting and neither is Ryan." She leaned closer. "Who do you think has been keeping him company all this time, huh? I know what he needs, and I've given it to him."

April stepped back. "Wh-what are you saying?" Her stomach churned a little, the beer not settling well after hearing this disturbing news. Hadn't she worried about this very thing? And did she have any cause to be jealous when she was the one who'd let him go?

"I'm saying, go the fuck back home, bitch." Shelby's head and shoulders rocked back and forth, emphasizing her words. "Ryan is mine. So head to your Barbie mansion, with your fucking purple cars, and dick-less Ken dolls and leave the *real* men to me."

Barbie mansion? Purple cars? She didn't have a purple car. Plus this woman was a bit delusion. "Ryan is *not* yours."

"Oh, but he is. Every fucking inch of him. And I mean every inch." Shelby held her fingers about twelve inches apart right in front of April's nose. "You think he's waited around for your candy ass?" She stabbed her black nail against April's breastbone. "No, he's been fucking me and every other piece of ass he could get his hands on for the past three years."

April considered grabbing the girl's finger and twisting it behind her back, because all the poking was entirely uncalled for. "I don't believe you."

"I don't care what you believe." Shelby's hands were working as wildly as the rest of her body now.

Her actions were just like the women on the reality TV shows April watched sometimes. The women got all crazy with their hands and words before the hair pulling and slaps began.

"I've had him for three years." Shelby pointed a finger at herself. "I'm not giving him up."

April hadn't fought to be with Ryan only to be blocked by this woman. She would fight for the man she loved. She wouldn't pull hair though, because she'd taken self-defense classes. This conversation was actually quite ridiculous but exhilarating, too. Her first girl-fight. She could do this. "Ryan has not had sex with you." At least, April hoped those words were true. "He said you're friends."

"Friends do fuck sometimes, princess." Shelby rolled her eyes and braced both hands on her hips. "And he's been fucking me into the mattress for months. I can give him what he wants. Down and dirty, but not you and your prissy self. You'll never please him."

April swallowed hard, because that was a high-probability due to her virgin status and all. Still… "You lie."

"No, see that's where you're wrong." Shelby stepped into April's personal space, her finger wagging madly again. "*Men* lie. They deceive. They make you believe in them. Fall in love with them and then they take it all away, but no I won't let him."

"Ryan doesn't lie."

"He's the biggest liar of all." Shelby shoved her shoulder,

Anger shot to the top of April's head like a mercury thermometer in the sun. All the pokes and prods of this woman's hands, not to mention the foul words spewing from her mouth pushed any sympathy out the window.

"And you, you Barbie-doll bitch, *you* are nothing. You think you can just show up here and take Ryan away from me." Shelby punched April's shoulder. "I don't think so."

Wincing from the blow, April shoved her back. "I *do* think so."

"Really, then where have you been for three years, huh? Cause I know where I've been, and it's in his bed, dirtying up the sheets. You need to leave, before I make you leave." Shelby's eyes narrowed into slits and she rubbed her fisted hand.

April clenched her jaw and braced her legs apart. "I am not going anywhere. It's taken me a long time to get here and I'm staying."

"You think you get to decide?" Shelby shouted. "You think you can come here and disrupt Ryan's life? He doesn't want you here. He's leaving. You know that, right? And he's taking *me* with him."

April knew the direction of Ryan's life and her part in his future. Something she'd yet to share with him, but she wouldn't discuss that with this irrational woman. "I know everything about Ryan, and I know you aren't going anywhere with him. I'm sorry you're hurting, but your words are simply not true."

"You don't know anything," Shelby shouted again. "You don't know the feel of his skin against yours, his heated kisses, his dick as it slides home. You don't know shit!"

Those words hit April right in the gut. Maybe Shelby *had* slept with Ryan, maybe she still was? So where did that leave her?

No. This woman would *not* put doubt in her mind. April loved Ryan, and if this woman wanted a fight, she'd soon learn that Barbie's could throw down.

# # #

Five minutes to closing time, Ryan flipped off the hot water tap, his glass-cleaning water was now at the right level in the bar's sink. He'd texted their newest employee to come down and wash the dishes. Over the past two weeks, Ryan had stayed after work to teach the kid a few tricks because the young guy wanted to be a bartender not a waiter.

After adding the sanitizing tablet, he heard Bane shout. He crumpled the sanitizer's wrapper in his hand and scanned the bar. "What the fuck?"

Bane was usually pretty chill...until you pissed him off. Scanning the bar, Ryan caught sight of the big guy. His face was bright red, the tendons in his neck visible, and Shelby was the recipient of the words roaring from his mouth.

April stood beside him, fisting her hands at her sides.
Oh no!

Ryan shot down the bar, lifted the pass-thru, and stopped at his friend's side.

"She's starting shit," Bane growled out, his beefy hand gripping Shelby's forearm. "I told you, man."

Ryan sidestepped, shielding April from Shelby. He clasped both April's hands in his. "Hey, it's okay."

She nodded and took a deep breath. "I'm sorry."

He tipped up her chin. "Don't apologize."

She gave a little nod, but lowered her gaze to their locked hands. "I-I can go."

"You're not going anywhere." Stubborn woman. He squeezed her hands and sighed when she didn't look at him. He'd deal with her worries once he cooled Shelby's temper. Ryan faced his friend. "What are you doing, Shelby?"

"What am *I* doing?" Shelby's jaw dropped and her eyes practically bugged out of her head. "What are *you* doing? She's a fucking fluff pot who speaks like she's some character in classic literature."

Bane groaned and leaned against a wooden pillar.

"I know who she is and how she speaks, so what's the real problem?" Ryan kept his tone calm and low so as to not draw even more attention to their little tête-à-tête. "I've told you about April, and I made clear we could only be friends. I know you're surprised she's here. But if you're mad at someone, be mad at me. I think you should go home. We can talk tomorrow."

"Ryan." April clasped his bicep.

"She wasn't real before." Shelby fisted a hand against her chest. "She never existed until now. *I've* been with you, and she doesn't get to come here and fuck that all up."

"I never said she would interfere with our friendship."

"But she is," Shelby cried. "I can see it in your face."

"Ryan!" April shoved between him and Shelby. "Let me handle this, please."

Bane chuckled.

Ryan shot him a glare. *Sure, jackass yuck it up!* "What? No." He ran a hand through his hair. In a way, he deserved this public flogging. He'd known how much Shelby loved him, but instead of breaking their ties, he'd remained her friend.

April narrowed her eyes and pressed against his shoulder until he moved. "I can fight my own battles now. Please don't interfere."

He could see the determination in April's eyes. The deep blue, begging him to step aside and see her as whole and capable of standing on her own. *Fine, then.* Maybe if Shelby got a glimpse of April's real strength, she'd understand why he loved the "fucking fluff pot."

April faced Shelby. "I believe you've misunderstood Ryan's attentions."

"Who the fuck talks like that?" Shelby glanced at him then at Bane.

Bane simply shrugged his lumberjack-sized shoulders.

April cleared her throat. "Shelby, I understand you've been friends with Ryan, and I can certainly understand the attraction." She flicked a hand in his direction. "To him and his...well, his attributes."

Attributes? He may have preened a little.

Bane rolled his eyes. "I just threw up a little."

Ryan punched his shoulder.

April glared at them both before turning back to Shelby. "I did leave Ryan. You are correct. I wanted him to explore his opportunities." April winced. "His *educational* opportunities."

The whole display was almost comical as April stood almost a foot taller than Shelby. Like some school marm scolding a student. And like a wayward child, Shelby was unpredictable and on the verge of throwing a fit.

"Oh, Ryan was exploring. Believe me." Shelby flashed a smug smile.

"What?" Ryan blinked then held up a hand, as if trying to block the words from flinging through the air. "Excuse me?" Three years he'd gone without sex. That deserved a gold star of some sort, not these lies. "Have you lost your—"

"Quiet." April slashed a hand between them. "I won't ask you again." Her eyes flashed and her lips were pursed into a perfectly kissable formation.

Fierce April did wicked things to his libido. Ryan arched a brow and mimed zipping his lips closed. He should throw April's sweet ass over his shoulder and carry her out of this bar. That'd end this bullshit argument. He'd never fucked Shelby, and he'd make that clear to Ms. Bossy-pants-school-marm-fluff-pot later.

"Shelby." April crossed both arms over her chest. "I'd like you to stop lying about Ryan."

He stepped closer to April and wrapped his arm around her waist. Her body was shaking a little. Hoping to calm her, he leaned over and kissed her temple.

Shelby released a pained whimper, staring at him as if he'd shot her straight in the heart.

Shit.

"That's it." Eyes narrowed, Shelby plowed forward and kicked his knee.

Losing his balance, he fell to the side, taking April with him.

He landed on one knee and reached for her, but couldn't halt her descent.

She plummeted to the ground, the right side of her head bouncing against the concrete floor.

The loud thump fired through his ears.

April screamed—an animalistic half-shriek, half-moan.

Bane shouted something then pulled away a kicking and screaming Shelby.

Ryan scrambled toward April.

Chest heaving and tears falling from her eyes, April held a shaky hand over her ear. Then she pulled away her hand and lifted it in front of her face as if peering at an alien being.

Blood. Her hand was covered in bright red blood.

"Oh, holy shit. Holy shit, April, tell me. Where is that

coming from?" Heart thumping and throat tight, he tilted her head to the side. Had she bashed open her head? "Baby, where's it hurt?"

"My new implant." April blinked, her voice barely above a whisper. "It's damaged."

CHAPTER 6

"What was April doing brawling in a bar?" Paul David paced around the emergency room waiting area. For the first time ever, Ryan saw the man in jeans and a navy-blue T-shirt. Cheri was sitting at Ryan's side in yoga pants and a flowy bright pink top. She and the senator had obviously grabbed comfortable attire and headed for the hospital after Ryan called.

Local news stations had caught wind of the story, so David's "handlers," had breezed in and attempted to find the perfect angle to placate the media hounds.

Bane had been the one to notify them of the impending publicity storm, because he had text alerts from a local TV station on his phone.

Breaking news: Senator Paul David's reclusive daughter injured in bar fight.

Ryan ran a hand over his dry mouth, prepared to accept all the blame. April had been in his presence one fucking day, and she was already injured. Three years she'd gone without a scratch, and after a couple hours with him, she'd landed in the ER.

David stormed past his public relations people, who were working furiously to draft a statement and stopped right in front of Ryan. "Do you have *any* idea what April went through to have her bilateral cochlear implantation? The delicacy the surgery took.

41

Who knows if this revision surgery will even work?" David threw up his hands before planting them on his hips. "And all because *your* jealous ex-lover had a break down."

"Paul." Cheri shifted forward in her seat, holding out a hand. "Please, sit for a moment."

"No, I don't want to sit. And I don't want to calm down." He glared at Ryan. "The doctors specifically said to *avoid* head trauma, and what does she do?"

The senator stared at Ryan as if he expected an answer. Ryan's father had never been a part of his life, so he wasn't clear on how to act or what to say or anything really. He'd never felt more chastised or defeated. "Well, sir, she—"

Paul flicked up a hand, halting Ryan's words. "She runs off and gets in a bar fight two months after the procedure, that's what she does."

Ryan wouldn't argue the ex-lover statement, because why would the senator believe him. He knew the kind of man Ryan had been three years ago. A player. A bad boy out for fun. Made sense that he'd believe Ryan would have lovers while at Harvard.

"Shelby wasn't Ryan's lover, Sir." Bane piped up. He'd stayed by Ryan's side, full of his own guilt over April's injury, and Ryan couldn't be more grateful.

Sitting in a waiting area filled with bleeding, crying, and screaming people was not how he'd envisioned tonight ending. He'd pictured two glasses of red wine and he and April discussing their future along with a love-making session in his bed. But now, she might have irreparable damage to her ear.

He still didn't know why she hadn't told him about the surgery. Apparently, she'd had cochlear implants placed in both ears. The Senator had explained that having a device in each ear made hearing speech from both sides of the head more easily processed by April's brain. Hearing with two ears also allowed her the ability to combine and compare signals from each ear, and her brain would filter out what she was trying to hear from what she was trying to ignore. This all made sense as Ryan could barely hear in a crowded room himself.

Sick to his stomach *and* sick in his heart, Ryan heaved a sigh and braced both elbows on his thighs. The look of sheer terror in April's eyes right before she'd passed out was one he'd never forget. A look he'd put there because he'd not been clear enough with a friend. But he'd never wanted to be cruel to Shelby. Even now he had conflicted feelings. But she owed April a huge apology, and if she couldn't do that then he'd be forced to end their friendship.

"Senator David." An officious looking man in blue scrubs stood by a door that led into the surgery area.

"Yes." April's father scurried over to the doctor, holding out his hand.

After introductions, everyone crowded around.

"April is recovering. However, please be aware certain complications can occur during the reinsertion operation. The possibility of differences in sound quality and speech recognition performance can exist with a replacement device, but"—he held up a hand—"speech perception ability will typically remain the same or improve. Luckily, we did not need to drill the cochleostomy site. April's device was simply jostled. The reconnection was quite simple, and though April may experience a bit of pain in the coming days, her implant is fine."

"Thank you doctor." David shook the man's hand. "When can we see her?"

"Let her sleep. She'll need an overnight stay at the very least. Also, I'd suggest making a follow-up appointment with her audiologist in two-weeks."

Ryan took a couple steps to the side and sank into the cold metal chair.

Bane slapped Ryan's knee as he sat down beside him. "Let me get you some food or something to drink."

While Ryan barely understood half of what the doctor had

said, he'd concentrated on what he *could* understand. *Her implant is fine.* "I've hurt her again."

"No, Shelby did that."

"I could wring her neck."

"She's always been a little off, man."

"I should've skipped work and dragged April to my apartment then none of this would have happened."

"Can't keep that woman locked up forever. Don't think April wants that." Bane lightly punched his shoulder. "I like her. Actually, I like her for me, so if you want to give her up, I'll take her."

"Fuck that." Ryan shot him a glare.

"That's better." Bane chuckled.

"Quit hovering, I'm okay. And yeah, a coffee would be nice. I need to find a way to see her."

"There is no *need*, only do."

Ryan rolled his eyes.

"Go charm a nurse, I'm sure she'd take you to see April." Bane lifted his big frame out of the too-small chair and stuck out a hand.

Ryan stared at his friend's open palm. "What?"

"Money."

"*Let me get you something to eat, Ryan*," he grumbled, mocking Bane's voice.

"I do *not* sound like that."

"No, you sound like an asshole." Ryan shook his head as he pulled out his wallet and handed Bane a stack of ones he'd acquired from the tip jar. "Coffee. Black, and hurry the hell up, and if they have any of those vanilla sandwich cookies, get me some of those."

"Will do." Bane held out his fist.

Ryan gave him a bump and watched him take off for the vending machines. "Hey, Bane."

His buddy turned around.

Ryan rubbed the back of his neck. "Thanks...for...you know."

Bane smiled and gave him a salute.

Hell, Ryan hated saying nice shit. But Bane had been there for him not just tonight but throughout his entire three years at Harvard. This was what April did to him. Turned him into a sap, expressing feelings meant to stay buried deep inside. He needed do to something. All this waiting was killing him. Determined in his course, he stormed over to where the senator sat beside Cheri. "I need to see April. Even if only for a minute, please."

Cheri studied him then nodded. "Paul." She clutched her husband's arm. "See what you can do. I know how convincing you can be."

"Flattery will get you everywhere." David kissed Cheri's cheek before walking to the nurse's station. After a couple minutes, he returned with slight smile. "The nurse will take you to her for just a short moment."

Ryan breathed a sigh of relief. "Thank you."

Cheri took his arm. "Give April a kiss for me."

"I will."

A gray-haired nurse, wearing light blue scrubs and sporting a stethoscope around her neck, came to his side and led him down the brightly lit hall to a room. All hospitals had the same smell—a pungent mix of cleaning products, urine, vomit, burnt flesh, and the metallic twang of blood.

After rounding a corner, the nurse opened the second door, and there April lay. Hooked up to all kinds of machines with lights flashing. Her blonde hair was strewn across her pillow. A yellow stain covered her neck from some disinfectant most likely and a big bandage covered her right ear. Long lashes rested against her pale cheeks. Her chest lifted with one breath at a time. As he stepped closer, he fought back the urge to kiss her awake. He settled for taking her hand and kissing it gently. "I'm so sorry. I never wanted you to end up like this. So many times I wanted to give up studying and come back to Indiana. And to you. But I kept going, because I had an end goal. However, being beside you in bed *this* way was not at all what I envisioned." He pressed her hand against his cheek. "Please be okay. I have too much I need to say to you, and we have our future to plan. No matter what happens with your...hearing, I'll be right here. I've always seen you as the strong one, don't change that now."

The nurse, who'd remained at the door, cleared her throat.

"Will someone watch her? She has nightmares and she'd feel better if I stayed with her."

"I understand, but I'm sorry. She needs rest." The nurse flashed him a smile she'd probably used to placate people for years. "You shouldn't even be back here now."

"Why do hospitals have these rules? She doesn't like new places. And she has issues with germs."

"Our rules are in place for a reason." The nurse opened the door and waved a hand toward the opening. "I'm sorry, but I can't let you stay."

Ryan remained at April's side, throat clogged with far too much emotion. "I just got her back. Please?"

The nurse came to his side and pressed a hand on his shoulder, her brown eyes reflecting her true sympathy. "We'll get her settled in a room, and then I'll send a nurse to get you."

"I understand." Ryan stood, leaned over, and kissed April's cheek. "It's just...we have so many things left unsaid, and I love her."

"I can see that." The nurse patted his cheek.

For the first time in...well, ever, he missed having a mom, or someone to hold him, guide him, and reassure him when his heart hurt so much. Not that he missed *his* mom, but what that word represented. Instead of breaking, he took a deep breath and smiled at the nurse. "Thank you for your kindness."

She blinked, then her face split into a big grin. "Oh, she'll have her hands full with you. Now, say goodbye to her, son."

Glancing down at April's still form, he shook his head. "I've never said good-bye to her. Never will." He kissed April's lips this time. "See you soon. We've got a lot to discuss, so quit lounging around."

The nurse chuckled. "That's the spirit."

"Tough love's the only thing that works with this one." Ryan jerked a thumb at the personification of trouble, wrapped in a thin white sheet. "She drives me insane."

"Well, good for her. Good for her."

Ryan grunted, took one last look at the woman lying on the bed, and followed the nurse back down the hall.

CHAPTER 7

Ryan scrubbed a hand over his face. Bane better have his coffee. He needed a jolt.

The nurse had gone back to her station after she'd pointed him in the direction of the waiting area.

He pressed open the door, took two steps, and then jarred to a stop when Dr. Ashburn barreled up to him.

Eyes narrowed, the man grabbed his shirt. "What have you done to her?"

Bane appeared behind the crazed man, holding a steaming cup of coffee. "Sorry, he's a tad unsettled."

Ryan nodded at Bane. "I got this."

"No *you* don't. You've hurt her again." Ashburn shoved against his chest. "I advised against this trip, but she was adamant about seeing through with this farce."

Ryan arched a brow and took a deep breath. The guy cared about April. Had helped her. He needed to remember that, but if Ashburn pushed him again…all bets were off. "First off, keep your hands to yourself. Second, April and I have a lot of unfinished business, and you know this. No way you've been talking to her all this time and she hasn't mentioned our future."

"Is that what you think?" Ashburn released a smug laugh and lifted his chin, meeting Ryan's gaze. "She came here to say goodbye. Her *future* is with me. I won't hurt her or put her in dangerous situations, unlike you."

Fighting off a wince at the truth of that statement, Ryan focused on remaining calm. The nurses were giving them the eye. Everyone in the waiting area had enough stress. They didn't need front row seats at an emergency room fight night. "Listen." Ryan lifted a hand between them. "I get that you're infatuated with her."

"Infatuated?" Ashburn scoffed. "I've been at her side through everything. From the very beginning. This trip was for her to close a chapter in her life, and now that she's seen what happens when she's with you, she'll be even more willing to shut the book. The two of you don't suit. The very idea is ludicrous."

Ryan raked a hand through his hair. When he'd first met April, sure, he'd agree the idea of being in a relationship with a socially awkward, wary, and slightly odd woman *was* ludicrous. But their broken pieces fit together to form a whole and nothing would keep them apart. If April had come to say good-bye, which he didn't believe, then this guy had brainwashed her somehow.

Bane bumped past Ashburn and handed Ryan his coffee. "Bro, I'll be right over there." He pointed to a chair set in front of the nurse's station. "Dude's playing you."

"Wait." Ryan took a long sip of hot, liquid gold. *Ah, caffeine.* "Better take this. Might get spilled."

Bane arched a brow then looked at Ashburn. "I got your back."

Ryan nodded. "S'all good."

"Better be." Bane narrowed his eyes at Ashburn. "Chill out, guy." Shaking his head, he lumbered over to the chair.

Ashburn watched Bane until he settled, and then he eyed the door behind Ryan. "I need to see April."

Ryan braced his legs apart and crossed both arms over his chest, because *hell no.* "I just came from visiting her. She's resting and doesn't need you back there." Plus she was basically unconscious. No way Ashburn was going back there while she was helpless. Fucking perv might touch her or do some weirdo shit.

Ashburn sniffed. "Forgive me, but you don't know anything about April's health."

Allrighty then. His last nerve left the building. Ryan stepped toward Ashburn, finger lifted between them. "I don't know what you *think* is going on between you and April, but I know her feelings aren't anything but gratitude."

The doctor sighed long and deep and then shook his head. "She was worried about this."

Ryan's brow furrowed. "Worried about what?"

"She does care for you, Mr. Cole. Very deeply, but over the past three years, she came to understand her feelings for you are only that of friendship. You are two very different people." The doctor smoothed a hand through his slick hair. "These past three years, I've had her on a bit of a five-step program. Each step made her stronger, but we've saved you for last. She knew this would be the hardest, because she knows how you feel about her, but she understands the necessity of letting you go." He huffed out a half-laugh. "Although, you've made this last step quite easy, as she'll see how unsafe you are. I'll be taking care of her now. You're no longer needed."

Oh, Mr. Fake-Freud was good. Very good. A thousand bees now swarming in his stomach good. And doubt, that little fucker, had broken free of the swarm and was now buzzing around in Ryan's brain. He inhaled deeply. "I'll believe your claims when I hear the words from April. Now if you'll excuse me, I need to get back to Cheri. I imagine she's curious about April's condition." Past ready for this little session to be over, Ryan stepped around the man and silently dared him to make a break for the door. *Please, go for it so I can drag your ass from the building. Please, give me a reason.*

"It'd be best if you just left." Ashburn grabbed his arm.

Ryan stiffened and glanced at Bane.

His buddy stood and headed in his direction. "Ryan?"

Seeing the big guy hustle forward must have knocked some sense into the man, because he released his grip.

"April came here to wish you well and close a chapter, that is all. She plans to return to Indiana. To me. She and I have discussed this for months since I revealed my feelings for her."

Did April's parents know her therapist had crossed a line? Why hadn't April mentioned she was having issues with this guy?

April *had* said she needed to speak with him. What about? Was she leaving him for her therapist? No. She'd stood strong against Shelby and claimed him as her own. *He* wasn't the one who was delusional. Steeling his spine, he straightened his too-tired body and faced Ashburn. "I'm not arguing about this anymore. I'm tired and one step away from pounding my fist into something. So unless you want to volunteer, back the fuck off."

Bane clasped a hand on his shoulder. "Ryan, let's—"

"You are nothing but a brute." Face red, Ashburn jabbed a finger against Ryan's shoulder. "You were wrong for her three years ago and you're wrong for her now. You are violence and deception. A wolf pretending to be a sheep." He threw up his hands. "She knows who and what you really are, and so do I."

Ryan stared at the spot the man had poked and breathed slowly through his clenched teeth. *Don't hit him. Don't.* "I have no idea what you're talking about. And we are in a goddamn waiting room, so settle your shit." Ryan basically shouted the words, but then he felt Bane's hand squeeze his shoulder, which grounded him, so he dropped his voice to more of a whisper-growl. "You are a psychiatrist, therapist, or what the fuck ever, so you should know better than anyone, no one in this waiting area needs to watch you lose your mind."

"I will not remain calm. I came here to fight for April's future." Ashburn lifted his fisted hand and shook it between them. "You just don't like hearing the truth."

51

Ryan half turned away from the man, because the guy was about to see what a 'wolf' could really do.

"I remember how brutal you were with her. I remember every cruel word you used. I also recall quite clearly how upset she was when she discovered how you plotted against her with her father."

"Enough!" Clenching his jaw, Ryan spun around. "*I* helped her. *I* pulled her out of the trenches when you and everyone else wished to keep her buried. *I* set her free."

"She's not free. She's in a hospital bed!" Spittle flew from Ashburn's mouth as he screamed down the walls. "I will not tolerate your interference in her life. She will do as I say, you will see."

And with that ominous warning, the guy turned on his heel and stormed to the exit.

Fury firing through his blood, Ryan took two steps forward then stopped. He couldn't beat the shit out of a guy in the middle of a hospital…wait, actually he could, as the guy would receive immediate treatment for the many blows to his know-it-all face.

Bane bumped his shoulder. "Guy's unhinged."

"Slightly." Ryan huffed out a nervous laugh. "He's wrong. About her. About everything. She's here for me. He lies." Who was he trying to convince Bane or himself? Damn the man for the wolf analogy, and the fucking bees in his stomach, and the stupid five step program that had probably led April to delusion-land.

"Yeah, he's a master-manipulator. He knows how to mess with the mind." Bane turned Ryan around. "Listen to me. Don't let his words dig into your head." He tapped Ryan's temple.

"I'm not."

"Yeah, you are."

Yeah, he was.

CHAPTER 8

April blinked awake then bit her bottom lip. Had the entire right side of her face been hit with a sledgehammer? Her heartbeat thumped in time with the throbbing in her temple.

Beat, beat.

Beat, beat.

She closed her eyes again, but not quickly enough, because nausea decided to pay a visit. Groaning, she twisted to her left side and bent her legs, trying to hold everything together. As she turned, she winced as light from somewhere blasted across her still-closed eyes. "Ah, too much light." She lifted a hand and placed it over her eyes.

"I'll fix that." A familiar voice replied, but not the one she wanted to hear.

Squinting, she watched as Dr. Ashburn closed the room's blinds, and then he closed the door, sealing her in.

Great. Sighing, she glanced around the room and then closed her eyes again, fighting off the dizziness and the pain. Last night's events played like movie frames behind her eyelids. The bar. Shelby. The fight. Ryan. Her fall.

No. She would not fall. Would not! She'd come here, because she'd climbed back to the top. She had a mission and it did not entail her lying broken on the ground. Well, she *was* broken again, but as always, she'd shove the pieces back together. So far, nothing had gone as planned, and the only words between her and Ryan were placed there by someone else.

Where was he?

She'd haul her sorry butt from this bed to find him if he didn't show up soon. She almost laughed. Here she'd made him wait three years and now she was as impatient as a five-year-old at Christmas. But Ryan Cole was one hell of a present, and she wanted to open him up and play with him…okay…that was sort of naughty, but true. She giggled.

"April? What's funny? Are you all right? Can I do anything else for you?" Dr. Ashburn approached the side of the bed and placed his hand against her arm.

Slowly cracking open her eyes, she studied the bandage covering a small wad of cotton on the top of her left hand. "What happened? Was my implant damaged?"

"Yes."

"Oh." Her stomach churned again, and she didn't voice the question now foremost in her mind: was the damage irreparable? "May I have some water? My throat hurts."

"Of course." He poured a small amount of water into a clear plastic cup, and then he lifted the straw to her lips. "Are you in pain?"

Straightening a little, she wrapped her lips around the green bendy straw and sighed as the cool water poured down her throat, easing the dryness. She licked her lips and took the cup from Gregory's hand. "Thank you."

He nodded then placed a hand against her forehead. "What else can I do?"

"Where is my father?" Not the question she wanted to ask, but mentioning Ryan around Dr. Ashburn usually resulted in a lecture and her head, brain, heart, and basically her entire body hurt too much to listen.

"He's gone to grab coffee with…with Cheri. Plus he said he

had an important phone call to make."

Barely holding her eyes open, April pulled the sheet higher against her chest. "I'd like some caffeine too." What she really wanted was to be alone. To gather her thoughts. Consider her next steps. Steps Gregory didn't agree with, but she'd take them anyway. His insistence on an intimate relationship between them made her uncomfortable in his presence. He'd helped her through so much, but that was his job, and she hated feeling as if she owed him more. Plus, hadn't she assisted in her own recovery? Hadn't Ryan? She *was* grateful to Dr. Ashburn, and she *did* love him, but only in an as-my-doctor sort of way.

"Would you like me to get you some tea?" He brushed her hair off her forehead.

"Oh, please, don't touch me. My head hurts so bad." She closed her eyes and slowly turned away. She did hurt and didn't like people touching her. He knew this. She'd fought past that phobia, but right now, her entire body was tense and her fear and severe pain were creating a black shroud over her will to fight. "I would love some tea and if you'd speak to a nurse about something for this pain, I'd be grateful."

"I'll text your father and ask him to bring you some tea."

Which meant he wasn't leaving, she sighed and couldn't help her next words. "Is Ryan with him?"

Dr. Ashburn released what sounded like a tsk. "April."

She lifted one eyelid. *Here comes the lecture.* That's all she needed to add to this invisible creature that seemed to be boring into her head. *Someone please save me.* Preferably Ryan with a huge cup of Earl Grey and a handful of Advil.

"After the events of last night, I'd hope you'd see reason." Gregory heaved a long sigh. "The man is not a healthy addition to your life. You're here only one day, and he put you in a situation in which you were grievously injured. I hold to my stance regarding your infatuation. It's not conducive to your recovery in any way. I hate saying I told you so…but because of him, you are once again suffering a setback."

"I don't wish to argue with you." Nor did she wish to listen to his condescending tone. "I'd just like an answer to my question. Is Ryan here?"

Gregory dropped his gaze to his phone and tapped out a message. "He's with his friend."

"Shelby?"

Ashburn glanced at her then back at his phone before clearing his throat. "Yes, I'm sorry."

April frowned. "Was she injured too?"

"I have no idea." Ashburn sniffed.

Something seemed very off. He wouldn't hold her gaze. "I'd like my phone, please."

After stuffing his phone in his front pocket, Ashburn clasped both hands behind his back. "April, let's get you healthy again before you delve into any more emotional…I'll call it…distress. Ryan is *not* here, but I am. I don't believe he provides the security you need. He has chosen to deal with his…friends rather than remain at your side. I feel you should consider that before calling him and begging an audience."

Was that the case? Was she begging for Ryan's attention when he was preoccupied with someone else? No. Cheri had warned her that the doctor knew just what to say to trigger her fears and doubts. The man did know her well. Too well. How unfair he'd use all that knowledge against her. "I understand you don't want me to speak to Ryan, but you've misjudged him. And *I* don't like being manipulated."

"I'm not the one manipulating you." He placed a hand against his breastbone. "His type uses people to get what they want. He *has* deceived you before."

"Yes, he has, but you are doing the same." Hadn't she said she didn't want to argue? And yet, here they were and she hated it. Once again, he was making her doubt herself and her feelings. Not to mention, the whole brain boring issue which wasn't improving with this conversation.

"I most certainly am not manipulating you. I am counseling you as I've always done."

Out of patience, April took a deep breath, fully opened her eyes, and leaned forward. "I've explained time and time again that I do love you, and—"

"Wait. You love *him*?"

April gasped. Ryan stood by the door, two to-go cups in his hands.

"Is that why you came here?" His gaze held hers. "Did you come to tell me you're with him now?"

April straightened, heart racing and on the verge of passing out from the pain. How much had he heard? "Ryan, I—"

"No, April, I get it. It's fine." He turned on his heel and left.

The door slammed shut.

She panted out a breath. Then another.

The clock ticked on the wall.

Ashburn sniffed.

Stomach churning, April stared at the place where Ryan had stood only seconds before. "Wait." She had to get him back. Had to explain. "No! Ryan!"

"A man who loves you wouldn't continually walk away." Ashburn shook his head.

"Enough. Just stop." His smug words were not what she wanted to hear right now. April whipped the covers off the bed then halted as a wave of dizziness almost dropped her to her knees. "No." She gritted her teeth and headed for the door, grateful she wasn't hooked up to anything.

"April, your gown is open." Ashburn grabbed her arm.

"I don't care. Let me go." Frantic, she yanked free and bustled down the hall after Ryan.

CHAPTER 9

"Ryan! Please stop."

What the hell? Is she following me?

"Ryan, don't go."

His heart had halted then shattered when he'd entered the room and heard her express her love for Ashburn.

"Ryan."

"Stop. I just need quiet!" His words bounced along the corridor, and he wasn't sure if he was yelling at April, his thundering heart, or at the echo of her words to that dick-head Ashburn.

April grabbed his arm, and then crumpled to the floor.

"April. Damn it." He turned and placed the to-go cups on the floor.

"I think I'm going to be sick."

Her face was a shade of green he'd never seen before. He shot up and looked around for a wastebasket.

Too late.

She wretched over and over, and then moaned and balled up on the floor.

The smell hit him hard, and he could only stare for a second before a nurse bumped past him.

Another shot him a glare as they helped April to her feet.

She struggled a little. "Ryan. Wait, where's Ryan?"

"April, stop, you'll injure yourself." Unable to resist her pleas, he closed the distance between them and braced his hands on her shoulders. She was so pale and her entire body shook hard. He glanced at the nurse. "I've got her."

The woman frowned. "She needs to go back to her room."

"Okay. All right." He picked up the to-go cups and followed. One cup had a little vomit splatter, so he tossed it in the garbage basket next to a chair set in the hallway. Why was he taking this path? He should just leave, but he couldn't until he saw April safely nestled back in her bed.

Entering the room again, he prayed Ashburn wasn't there, because he didn't trust himself not to beat the shit out of the man.

After he settled in a metal chair, he set her tea on a table and waited. She loved another so that was it. That's why she was here. He'd lost.

April shuffled out of the bathroom, still looking a little pale and clutching the right side of her head. "Gross. I had to rinse out my mouth with the little bottle of Listerine."

The nurse guided her to the bed. "I'll have to hook you back up and give you more pain meds."

"I don't care." April flicked a hand at the machines. "I'd like a moment alone with Ryan."

The nurse nodded then looked at him. "Keep her in this bed. I'll be back."

After the nurse left, he stood. "You're settled now. I brought you some tea, so I'll go."

"Ryan, no." She panted out. "Please, you misunderstood. I-I don't love him. I wasn't saying it that way." She closed her eyes and visibly swallowed hard. "Please, don't leave me. Let me explain."

He should wait, let her rest, but he had to know. "You said, 'I do love you,' April. I heard it."

"I do love him." She opened her eyes again and winced. "Yes, I said that, but I don't love him like I love you."

Her eyes dripped with sincerity, and his heart started thumping normally again. Since she'd arrived yesterday everything was catawampus. They needed to sit down uninterrupted for longer than five minutes and talk.

Yet, here she lay, shivering in a pale blue hospital gown. Everything about this moment was too raw, and she wasn't the only one vulnerable. "April, now isn't the time. You're in so much pain, baby. Close your eyes and get some rest."

"No." She lifted a shaky hand toward him. "I-I can't until I know you believe me."

He took her hand and lightly squeezed her long, beautiful fingers. "I believe you."

She groaned and rolled her eyes. "Do not patronize me, Ryan Cole. You do *not* believe me." She tugged on his fingers. "I came here for you. I am ready for you. And no one. Not Shelby. Not Dr. Ashburn. Not my stupid ears. Nothing will keep me from you, and I mean it." With a slash of her hand, she flicked away the tears on her cheeks. "Th-the only p-person who can change my mind is you. So, tell me right now." She took a deep breath. "Tell me we don't want the same thing. Tell me you don't love me anymore."

"I'm not *telling* you anything."

Her eyes widened.

"I'll show you as soon as you get out of that hospital bed."

"Show me now."

"No. You need rest."

"I need you to kiss me."

"April, you can barely keep your eyes open. You just got sick in the hallway."

"Please, just one kiss, Ryan, then I'll know." She tugged on his hand. "I told you I used Listerine, so I won't taste like puke."

He chuckled and shook his head. "April—"

The nurse barreled into the room and handed over a couple pain pills before glancing at Ryan. "She needs rest."

"That's what I've been telling her."

April picked up the to-go cup. "What's in here?"

"Earl Grey."

She smiled, a tooth-revealing grin. "I love you more than mashed potatoes, and that's a lot."

The nurse chuckled. "Get some rest, April, and we'll see about getting you something to eat."

April nodded then pulled the lid off the tea and breathed in the scent. "Ah, just what I needed."

Seeing her joy stirred Ryan's cock a little. He really needed a more up to date visual of April in the throes of passion, but this would have to do until he had her beneath him again. Right now, he needed to be satisfied that she loved him, not Ashburn.

After she finished her tea, she faced him again. "Ryan, is my implant okay?"

"Yeah, the doctor said it was. Well actually, he said a bunch of stuff I didn't quite understand, but I did catch that your implant was fine."

Her brow furrowed. "Really?"

He stood and took her hand. "Yes, really."

"Okay." She yawned and then tugged on his upper arm. "Kiss me, please."

He leaned down and kissed her. What was meant to be a quick get-some-rest kiss turned into a release of all the longing he'd held too close for three long years. He kissed her like he'd die without her. Kissed her like a man finally letting go of each remaining shred of fear and uncertainty.

She moaned into his mouth, skating her tongue over his, and then she dug her fingers into his hair and pulled. Head tilted, she gasped and tried to bring him down on top of her.

"Whoa." Reluctantly, he eased away. Yet, unable to resist, he placed a few more soft kisses on her plumped red lips. "Not here. We'll get you discharged then I'll take you to my place and we'll talk. Uninterrupted. I have just as much to say as you do."

"I don't want to talk anymore." She licked her lips. "Like you said, I'd rather show you what I want." Her gaze dropped to where his dick strained against his pants. "And I know what I want."

His cock was already harder than hell, and April checking out his situation had him turning titanium. He bent and whispered in her left ear. "I've waited three years for you. Don't tease me now."

"Who says I'm teasing?" She cocked a brow.

He tapped a finger against her nose and pulled back from temptation before he explored all that skin beneath the flimsy gown. Her rosy scent shot through his senses, driving him crazy. Her ruffled hair. Her kiss-roughed lips. *Fucking hell.* "April, give a guy a break, would ya?"

"I'm not afraid anymore." She peered at him from beneath lowered lashes. "I want you…in every way."

Ryan clenched his jaw. His entire body throbbing with need. Though his dick disagreed, her first time would not be on a hospital bed.

"Ryan?" She blinked, once then twice. "Please don't leave. Dr. Ashburn…he…" She yawned again, patting her fingers over her mouth. "I don't have the energy to deal with him right now. His refusal to see reason is exhausting."

"I'd rather not talk about Ashburn, okay?" Ryan refrained from saying he'd kick the guy's ass if necessary, and he was starting to think it might be necessary. "Can you hear okay?" He brushed her hair over her right ear.

"Yes, but my head hurts like a stampede of wildebeests ran over my face, and my stomach and throat hurts from puking."

"I'm so sorry." He pressed his forehead against the back of her cool hand. "I should've stopped Shelby. I should've done a lot of things different. I never wanted you in pain like this."

"Wasn't your fault."

He sighed. "In a roundabout way it is."

April dropped her gaze. "Is Shelby your girlfriend, Ryan?"

"Look at me." With an index finger, he tipped up her chin.

"I've been too long without this face, so don't deny me. And no, Shelby is my friend. But, she's like your Dr. Ashburn. She doesn't understand us. And she has developed feelings for me. Feelings I don't return."

April nodded. "I believe you."

Ryan smiled and kissed her lips lightly when he really wanted nothing more than to devour her again. "April, please go to sleep."

"You'll stay with me."

"I *have* been with you. I left to get you tea."

"That's not what Gregory said." She frowned and flicked a glance at the door.

"I'm not surprised."

"I'm sorry you heard what you did, but the words were taken out of context."

"I know that."

She bit her lower lip. "But you left."

"I would've come back." Probably. Well, more than probably. He would've realized he was a fighter, and April was his, and he would've stormed back in here, challenging Ashburn to a duel or some stupid medieval shit.

She flashed a sly grin then wrapped her slim arm around his neck. "Would you have fought for me?"

"No." He ran a finger across her lower lip when it formed into a slight pout. "I would just steal you away."

"I like that idea." A sensual curve lifted her lips and a heat he'd never seen before twinkled in her eyes.

"April David, are you trying to seduce me?"

"I am."

Her words were a husky murmur that shot straight to his cock. He closed his eyes for a moment, fighting not to join her in that tiny bed and discover the truth behind her words. "April, while I like the direction of your thoughts, now is not the time."

"No?"

Needing to do something with his hands, other than hauling her up to him and kissing her senseless, he fiddled with her cover and pressed his lips against her forehead. Then he kissed her cheek before speaking in her left ear. "When you get out of here, I dare you to try your seduction again."

She opened her mouth to reply but the door opened and her father and step-mother walked in. She gripped Ryan's hand and squeezed. "I accept your challenge, and know this, I won't be *trying* anything."

Ryan smiled and then slumped into the metal chair before her father noticed his raging hard-on.

Shy April was apparently gone, replaced by this bold seductress. If she wanted to take the reins, he'd sit back and enjoy the ride.

Enjoy? Hell, he'd likely die, but what a way to go.

CHAPTER 10

Light streamed through the sheer white curtains. Ryan shifted on the bed and bumped into something. He blinked. April. No way in hell was she finally in his bed and he was *sleeping*.

They'd checked her out of the hospital around 11 a.m. the day after her fall, and he'd brought her to his apartment. Both exhausted, they'd undressed down to their underwear and tumbled into his king-size bed with promises to talk once they'd caught up on sleep.

He had no idea what time it was now. But she was still beside him, so that was all that mattered. He had morning-wood, or more likely late-afternoon wood, which had morphed into some kind of steel beam protruding from his body, if that was possible.

She'd said she was ready for intimacy, but she'd never had sex, so he wasn't about to take her like some barbarian claiming his spoils. Regardless of what they both wanted, they had to take these next steps slow. A gentle progression was how they'd proceed, and that was only after they'd discussed everything that needed to be said. He was leaving for a job in Maine after all, and whether she knew it or not, she was coming too.

April shifted in the sheets and then wrapped one arm and one leg around him.

Content in the moment, he fell back to sleep for a while.

Sometime later, when the light no longer poured through the window, he stirred awake at the soft press of lips against his shoulder, and a slight nudge of hips against his side. "Ryan, are you awake?"

"Yeah." He pulled April's hand up to his lips and kissed her fingers.

"All those times we spoke while we were apart...I believe that solidified our friendship, but now...I want more." She tugged on his shoulder so he turned to face her. "Tell me you feel the same."

He massaged her neck and shoulder until she purred like a spoiled cat. "Are you in pain?"

"My head and right ear do hurt a little, but I think our nap did me good." She lifted a hand and held it between them. "May I touch you?"

"Wait." He kissed her hand. "Let me get you some pain meds."

"No." She shook her head. "Don't leave. You'll spoil the moment." Trailing a finger down his chest, she stopped at the top of his boxer briefs. "I feel this heat between us, it's burrowed in my chest, and lighting up my thighs, and making me so wet, I can't stand it anymore. I've dreamed of the way you touched me, and I would wake up alone and I-I...well, I had to touch myself as I remembered how I exploded in your arms." She ran her index finger just under his waistband before tugging them down and off. "I want that again. I want your hands all over me. I want you to kiss me. To touch me. Fill me. Please, Ryan, I ache, so...tell me you want the same. Tell me you still love me."

Had he said something about steps? What steps? This kissing and touching idea seemed like a much better plan. "I'm not *telling* you anything, April David. I believe I said I'd show you." He pressed her back against the mattress, settled between her legs, and—

A knock sounded on his door.

What the actual fuck?

Ignoring it, because April's silky neck called for kisses, and his dick felt so good against her hip. "Mmm…you still smell like roses."

The knock turned into a pounding.

April gasped. "Who's that?"

Ryan growled out every curse word he knew, lifted slightly, much to the dismay of his dripping dick, and ran his fingers through his hair. "I am so done with this interruption shit." He kissed April's forehead. "Do not move." He stayed naked, because whoever was at his door needed to know exactly what they were interrupting so they'd turn the fuck around and leave. He stomped out of the bedroom, barreled down his narrow hallway, and whipped open the door. "What?"

Dewey stood on the other side, a grim look on his face. "Ryan." Nodding, he stepped inside.

His dick instantly deflated. *Damn it!*

April shrieked and then ran straight into the big guy's arms. Hadn't Ryan told her to stay in his bed? But no, she was wearing one of his T-shirts and her bright pink underwear was visible as she wrapped her arms around her pal. *Great.*

Leaving the door open, because Dewey *would* be leaving, Ryan braced both hands on his hips. "What the hell are you doing here?"

Dewey kept April in his beefy arms. "The senator called last night so I took the first flight out."

"Well nice to see you again, but I've got this now." Ryan waved a hand toward the door, because he did have neighbors across the hall, and he was standing with his dick out. Literally.

"Obviously you don't have anything under control." Dewey shook his head. "And will you please go put some clothes on."

"Oh, I'm sorry does seeing me naked offend you? Well then, leave! Come back in a couple days. I might be dressed by then." Done seeing his woman in another man's arms, Ryan scowled.

"April, come over here, please."

She unwrapped herself from her friend and came to his side. "Ryan, Dewey is worried about me. It's okay. I'm okay." She pressed her lips together then placed a hand in front of his crotch.

He glanced down at her hand then at her and raised a brow. "Placing your hand there will only make the situation worse."

"Oh." She laughed, but didn't move her hand.

"Yeah, oh." He shifted and his aching dick bumped against her cool fingers. "April, go back to bed, please." Had he done something to someone at some time to cause this ridiculous situation? Was his dick meant to be cold and shelterless forever?

"What happened?" Dewey stood in the middle of his living room, his hands on his hips.

Ryan started to answer, but April turned and placed her non-dick-blocking hand on his chest. "Let me explain what happened."

"April, can't you call him in a couple days? We have urgent business." He glanced down at his dick.

She grinned and then the little minx, brushed her fingers against his cock.

"Oh, hell no." He gripped the back of her neck and bent to take her mouth in a bruising kiss.

"Cole! Go put your dick in some pants. Fuck." Dewey wrenched April away and led her across the room to sit on Ryan's light-brown couch.

"Un-fucking-believable." Ryan knew he was pouting like a bitch, but he didn't care. "Make yourself at home, asshole. Grab a beer. Make a quiche. Whatever you want." He flounced off to the bedroom, threw on some shorts then rambled back into the kitchen for a beer, because this occasion called for something, anything to soothe his nerves. One way or another, he was getting Dewey out his door, and April back beneath him before anyone else interrupted.

Carrying two half-full glasses of filtered water and a cold beer bottle, he sank next to April on the couch. Her hands were flying all over as she relayed the story of her bar fight.

"...and my implant is fine, so we checked out of the hospital and came here."

"Good, I was worried."

April patted Dewey's knee. "Thank you for worrying, but I'm fine." She stood. "Ryan and I have...um...to talk about some things...so, um...can we visit more later."

Dewey looked at April then turned and glared at him. "I assume you'll be careful with her."

"I will be." Ryan returned the big guy's stare, not backing down because he knew Dewey's words held a double-meaning.

"Cole, you and I talked a lot three years ago, and we've touched based since then, so I get that you're doing this *thing* with April. But I feel I need to make something clear."

Ryan settled the cold beer bottle between his legs for a bit of relief, because a lecture was on its way.

"April has transformed herself. No more fear of germs, people, touch. She's fought so hard. She rarely has nightmares anymore. And while I know she did a lot of this for herself, she did it for you, too. So, I'll say this one more time. Don't fuck it up."

Ryan held out his fist.

Dewey bumped it.

"Big guy, you were there for her for a long time. I get that. I appreciate that. You loved her first and will love her always. So...I don't know...shit...just thanks. Thanks for being her friend. I'm not going to thank you for being here right at this *exact* moment, but I will in some not too distant future appreciate that you came to check on her. But, it's all good."

"I wouldn't say it's all good." April shrugged and ran a hand along her neck. "I do still have issues sometimes, and I do still take a few meds."

"We all have issues." Dewey shifted to the edge of the couch. "Don't get caught up in them."

"I will try." April nodded.

Dewey shot to his feet, plucked her from the couch, and embraced her. "I'm here now, so if you need me, I want you to call. And instead of *talking* to numb-nuts here, maybe you should be resting."

Ryan chuckled. He only wished his nuts were numb.

April's face flushed pink. "If you're trying to say I shouldn't have sex, I'm going to disagree with you. We've already had this discussion, Dewey." She snuck a quick glance at Ryan.

Dewey frowned again.

April shoved him toward the door. "I'm where I want to be, and everyone just needs to understand that and let me be now."

"Cole." Dewey pointed a finger. "I'm watching you."

"I hope not," he muttered.

Dewey took a step toward him, but April shook her head. "He's right," she giggled. "It's better if you don't watch."

Dewey's gaze shot to hers. "April David!"

"I'll see you later." With a cheeky grin, she hugged him again. "Thank you for coming. It means a lot, but I need you to go now."

Dewey nodded then turned back and faced Ryan. He forked two fingers, pointed toward his eyes, and then shot them toward Ryan and left.

"Yeah, yeah, I get it. You're watching." Ryan rolled his eyes.

April shut the door, and then leaned against it for a second. Head tilted, she studied him for a moment before lifting his T-shirt over her head, tossing it on the floor, and then walking her sweet ass back to his bedroom.

# # #

After he'd kissed her until she couldn't breathe, April heaved a sigh of relief. Now that they'd come to this moment, she felt a small trickle of uncertainty—not fear, travel down her spine. Would she be enough for him? Would sex hurt? Maybe a little. Cheri had explained, but she'd also said April should share her fears. Explain to Ryan her concerns so he could help her through her first time.

But she was anxious to get this done. Her entire body was hot and her core throbbed and she was so wet and achy. The smell of need and want circled through the air, making her dizzy with lust. She wanted to stay in this bed for hours, days, years, and learn everything about sexual pleasure.

"Are you really here?" Braced above her, Ryan gazed into her eyes, his brown eyes filled with a bit of something, maybe worry, maybe awe? "Are you feeling okay? Your ear is it…"

"I'm fine. A dull ache, but I've dealt with worse pain. I can tolerate anything except losing you." April ran a hand down his chest. "I want to marry you."

"Whoa." He held up a hand and sat back on his knees. "You don't get to ask me that. Let me wear the pants for once, please. I've been dancing on your string for three years, but that's over now. And if you don't believe me." He shoved off the bed. "I'll show you."

"Wait." She swallowed hard and clamped her thighs together. He was leaving. Now? "Where are you going?"

"I need my phone."

"Your phone?" She practically shrieked the words. Hadn't they stalled long enough?

"Yeah. You seen it?"

"No." But she could see his taut butt, his muscled thighs, and his tapered back. She harrumphed. A woman *could* ask a man to marry her. They weren't living in the 1950's for goodness sake. Not that she'd actually *proposed*, anyway. She'd suggested.

"My jeans." He lifted a finger in the air as if having a "eureka" moment then mumbled, "Wherever those are." He disappeared into the hallway.

Ryan looking for his phone reminded her of her phone—and her responsibilities. "Oh, no."

"What's wrong?" He returned, his gaze locked on his phone as his finger pecked at the screen.

"I need to call Britni. I was supposed to meet her today and I can't." She lifted up on her elbows. "My phone is in that plastic hospital bag. Can you grab it?"

"Sure." He left again before sauntering back in and handing over her phone.

She made the call to Britni, explaining her situation but guaranteeing her new friend she'd visit before she left the city.

"Everything okay?"

April frowned. "I feel really bad."

"I'm sure she understands."

"I suppose." April sighed.

"Look." Ryan tilted his phone in her direction.

A flight itinerary was on the screen.

To Indianapolis.

Set to leave tomorrow at 8:50 a.m.

"See." He rocked the phone back and forth. "I was coming to get you and planned to make a few declarations of my own."

Why would he think this information took precedence over love making after three long years? While she appreciated the sentiment, she had needs. Serious needs. Removing the phone from his hand, she placed it on his bedside table, which was littered with law books. "All right. You've shown me. Now can we continue?"

"Continue what?" He grabbed both her hands and lifted them above her head. "Mighty bossy, aren't we, Ms. David?"

She spread her legs to accommodate his presence, and maybe rub up against him a little. The feeling was quite pleasant so she did it again.

He chuckled and placed a finger on her kiss-slicked lips.

Lifting her head, she tried biting him. Feral. That perfectly described her feelings right now. She wanted to bite, and kick, and scream.

He growled and pulled away his finger, closing his eyes briefly. "How do you know you're ready for sex, April? How do I know? I can't handle you leaving me again or not trusting me. We need to come to an understanding before this goes much further."

"All right, if we must do this now," she huffed, her entire body still tingling. "Release me." She tugged on her hands still in his grip.

"My, my, someone's impatient." He quirked a cocky grin, hesitated for a moment, but released her arms yet maintained his position on his knees above her.

She narrowed her eyes. "Yes, someone is quite frustrated. Sexually. You do recall one of us is a virgin, ready to burst while the other is not? And apparently only one of us wishes to talk, which is ridiculous, because we could talk after the whole make-April-not-a-virgin experience."

"April."

His tone suggested his exasperation. "Fine. All right. Yes, let's have a chat first." She flipped her hair away from her face and planted her hands on the top of his legs before drawing small circles with her thumbs. "I didn't know myself *or* love myself before, but I spent the last three years fixing that. I forced myself into social situations, took online classes, worked on erasing my phobias and focused on who I wanted to become. I even did some counseling work with, Dr...um...Dr. Ashburn, and I'm proud of that." She heaved a long sigh. "Before you came along, I didn't understand how much I let my past define me. I want you to love who I've become. You know me and my entire past. I've told you things no one else knows. I've missed you every day"— she focused on his Adam's apple, avoiding his gaze—"but, I had to give you a choice."

"April, I didn't—"

"Shh...let me finish and don't interrupt, please."

73

"Bossy." He bent to kiss her.

"Nope." She turned her face to the side, avoiding his lips. "You wanted to talk so now you'll listen."

"God, I want you." His entire body shuddered. "Your whole bossy-fierce thing is hot as hell."

"Again, listen." She rolled her eyes. "I was giving my argument as to why I'm ready for sex."

"I don't think I care anymore." He dropped kisses along her jaw and down the side of her neck.

"I wasn't done." She shivered and nudged him with her shoulder. "I wanted you to have a choice. I didn't want you to be with me if you could find someone...better."

"Ap—"

"Shush." She pressed her index finger against his firm lips and tried not to become distracted when he kissed her finger. "I know lots of opportunities...and by opportunities, I do mean sex with other women, existed." Her stomach clenched at the thought of him with someone else. "I wanted to offer you more than a broken woman. I didn't want pity or guilt. I wanted you on my terms. Not yours. And not my fathers." She shifted beneath him, because here came the big part. The open-her-heart part. "I want to show you who I've become. I want to share my life with you now that I'm stronger and free from the past...and all my phobias." She huffed out a laugh, shaking her head. "Well...for the most part." Meeting his soft brown eyes, she felt she should be honest about her true mental state. "I'm not saying I don't have moments, but when I do, I think of you and I get through them." Throat clogged with emotion, she whispered her worst fear. "Am I too late?"

He gripped her chin. "Look at me."

Taking a deep breath, she prepared for whatever he might say.

"There were no other women."

Tears pooled in her eyes. "None?"

"You're not too late. I still love you." Brow narrowed, he squeezed her chin between his forefinger and thumb. "Don't doubt me again."

She burst into tears.

"Hey, hey, what's wrong?" He pulled her into his arms.

Blubbering. *Real attractive, April.* "I-I d-didn't think you being with other women mattered b-but it did and you used that tone on me and I hate it and I love it. And I'm so glad there was no one else. I couldn't stand it. I'm so sorry."

"Oh, April. Why didn't you just ask?" He shuffled off the bed and grabbed a tissue box from the side table. He tugged a couple pieces free and handed them over.

After wiping off her face and nose, she burrowed against his chest. "I imagined you with other woman. I even had nightmares about it, but I'd let you go, so if you sought another then it was my own fault."

"There weren't any others."

He'd stayed true. What a gift.

Lifting her chin, he kissed the tip of her nose. "How could there be others when you hold my heart?"

She sniffed and glanced up at him, very much done talking. "I don't want to leave this bed for days."

"Oh, my sweet, April. Believe me, you won't. You have years to make up." He lowered her back on the bed and kissed her.

All doubt and fear gone, she showed him in her kiss and her touch that she wanted him and only him. Uninhibited and finally free to reveal all the love in her heart.

CHAPTER 11

Kissing his way down April's body, Ryan got up close and personal with the hot pink rose tattooed on her right hip. His name was etched in black in the middle. And the date he'd left was scrolled underneath. *He* was imprinted onto her skin—a part of her forever, and he loved that she'd claimed him that way.

He wrapped his arms around her trim waist and kissed her tattoo. "Seeing my name on your skin does insane, animalistic things to me, April."

She hummed in agreement or in pleasure, he couldn't say.

But damn, that hum ripped through his already hard-as-hell cock.

"This date is when I left." He skimmed his finger along the rose. "I want you to get another for the date you returned."

Lifting up on her elbows, she met his gaze then nodded. A single tear slipped down her cheek.

"Once you get the new tattoo, everything will be complete. The beginning and the end, right?" He tucked her hair behind her ear, careful of the recently jostled device.

"Can I put a circle around both dates? Because we have no end or beginning, we just keep circling. Keep surviving. You and me against this crazy world." She smiled then tugged on his arm, and pulled him up her soft, silky body.

As he kissed her again, he realized this was what mattered. This tightness in his skin. This unending ache in his heart for her and only her. "I'll never let you go." He whispered the words against her left ear and whether she heard him or not didn't matter. The only thing that mattered was her grip on his body and her moans against his lips.

He could do this. Build her need up so high until she wanted to come so bad, she'd scream if she didn't find release.

But no matter how bad he wanted to claim her, he needed to make sure she was fully ready. He eased back. "April, for your first time, I'll do everything I can to make it pleasurable, but just know, we don't have to have sex right now. We have time, and we can do other things together. I'm happy to show you." He grinned and lightly kissed her lips.

"I know I have a lot to learn. I know losing my virginity might sting a little, but I want us to connect fully. I want to feel you moving inside me. You're the only one who's ever touched my heart and the only one who'll ever touch my body."

"Damn right."

She grinned and brushed a hand over his face. "I've fought for you and for me. If I had to endure everything I lived through in order to get to this moment, I would do it all again. I know I made you wait, but I needed that time. I needed to love me so I could love you. And this feeling inside my chest right now is overwhelming. Maybe we should talk more, maybe we should take steps, but I know this is the right moment for us."

Ryan closed his eyes as the love between them stirred in the air. So strong almost as if he could touch it. "This is it then, April David. You let me in all the way, and I won't let you turn back. You're mine, and I'm yours, and we're together until we're old and gray and holding hands as we dodder through the park. You hearing me?"

"I know I don't have the best hearing, but yes, I hear you. I feel you, and I love you." She grabbed the back of his neck and tugged him down. "Now show me."

He shifted to his side and pulled her against him, kissing her, practically losing his mind with each brush of their lips and swipe of their tongues. He couldn't get enough, and in order to delve deeper, feel more of her smooth skin, he eased over her and devoured her mouth until he couldn't breath. "I want to be your air. Your world. I want it all." Taking her hand, he placed it upon his chest. "Touch me as I touch you."

He ran his fingers over her peaked nipples and she did the same to him. They both hissed out a breath.

Trailing his fingers over her silky, flat stomach, he shivered as she did the same. "Now I want you to touch me."

She gripped his cock in her hand. Not tentatively, but apparently sure of what she wanted. "Like this."

"Oh, hell yes, like that." He fought back the urge to come then and there. His April was so brave. So fierce. "Take charge of that cock."

"You touch me, too." She bit her lower lip and glanced down her body.

"Fuck, I'm on fire." After sliding his hands along her inner thighs, he slid his index finger over her slick folds and then pressed his middle finger inside her wet core.

Her body jerked.

"Shh…shh…shh. It's okay. Look at me."

She met his gaze. "I want more."

He grunted. "Keep moving your hand on my cock."

"Oh, sorry. I was distracted." She crinkled her nose then gripped him again.

"S'okay." Wanting to reassure her, he bent and kissed her, working her mouth as they moved their hands in rhythm together.

Her hips lifted with each plunge of his finger, so he pressed his palm against her clit.

She moaned against his mouth. "Oh, that's so nice. I've

wanted this feeling for so long."

"I'm happy to give it to you." He kissed his way down to her nipple, licking the tip before teasing it with his tongue.

"Ryan, the sensations are too much." She gripped his head against her chest.

He kept a finger working inside her, but she'd released his dick. Likely too caught up in all her new feelings. Sliding a second finger inside her, he shifted his attentions to her other nipple. He pressed the flat of his tongue against it and then softly bit the hardened tip.

Hot, so damn hot.

Her body was flushed.

Her hair spilled across his pillow.

His visions of her hadn't done this moment justice.

Body shaking with need, he kissed and nipped his way down her stomach, keeping the plunge of his fingers slow and steady. Once above her core, he flicked his tongue against her clit then pressed down hard.

"Ryan, that's right. Yes, so right. Please. Oh, please, yes, don't stop."

One more swipe of his tongue, and she broke, back arching, and her throat releasing harsh breaths. Her whole frame jerked over and over. Her palm was in her mouth, and she was biting down hard. "No…no more."

He squeezed the base of his cock, watching her come had just about pushed him over the edge. His dick was shouting, hey, what about me?

After she stopped pulsing against his hand, he rose above her. "I'm going to kiss you now."

Her forearm was flopped across her face, but she quickly dropped it to the side and met his gaze. "B-but you were just down there… and I-I just…"

"That's right." He grinned and rubbed his cock against her stomach. "Sex is messy and dirty and we're doing it all."

She took a deep breath and nodded. "Okay, yes, kiss me."

And he did, delving deep, making her taste her own pleasure on his tongue.

She seemed hesitant at first, but soon she was writhing against him again. "Please, get inside me. I need more. I feel so empty."

He grabbed a condom from the side table drawer. "April, watch. See I'm protecting you."

"Do those hurt?"

"Well, they're a bit of a nuisance sometimes, but necessary. We aren't ready for baby Ryan's toddling around."

She smiled. "Oh, but they'd be so cute."

"No." He shook his head. "I shouldn't have brought up the subject. Babies can cause performance issues."

Tilting her head, she studied him for a moment then glanced at this cock. "I don't see any evidence of that."

"No?"

"No."

"Well, let's begin then." He rose above her, ready to express his love, his gratitude, and his overwhelming appreciation for her bravery. He kissed her. Long, sweet, deep and easy. With reverence. With all the pent up emotion in his soul.

She wiggled against him. "I love you too, Ryan."

He grinned, grateful she'd felt what he meant to express, and that connection with her brought a tear to his eye. "Fuck me, you are amazing." He grinned down at her. "I'm going to make love to you now, okay?"

"All right." April nodded. "Yes, please."

So sweet, he had to kiss her again. Just a quick peck on her lips. "Tell me if it hurts. We're taking this nice and slow."

"Thank you, Ryan, but honestly, I just want you inside me."

"Here we go." He set the tip of his dick at her entrance, and slid it in and out.

"More." Lifting her hips, she gripped his arms. "Stop teasing me."

Careful, so careful, he pressed a little deeper, slowly plunging into her body.

Three years he'd waited.

Oh, God, she felt amazing.

So slick.

So hot.

So his.

He wouldn't last long.

But he'd try.

For her.

Don't watch the slide into her body. Don't look at her pinked chest and plump red lips. And sure as hell don't look at his name tattooed on her hip.

"Fuck me." He rolled his hips against her.

"Oh my, you're very…um…filling." Eyes wide, she winced a little and shifted her hips.

He stopped. "You okay?"

"I'm okay." She blinked, but nodded. "Just a slight pinch, but I don't care. I need you to move. I have this ache and I think it'll go away if you make me come. So, please hurry."

"Easy baby." He lifted her hand to his lips and kissed it. "We'll take it slow."

"Fuck slow."

"Oh, April." His entire body shivered at her dirty word. "That sweet mouth saying bad things, are you trying to make me crazy?"

"Yes, I-I want you to fuck me. Just fuck me."

"Not this time." He clenched his jaw, because that's exactly what his body and dick wanted, but his heart and head said, calm your naughty-shit down and remember she's a damn virgin. "This time I'm making love to you but next time all bets are off."

She tried rocking against him, but he pressed a hand against her cheek. "Slow, baby."

Groaning, she ran her hands up and down his back. "Please, touch me. I'm almost there."

So was he.

Intense pleasure tingled at the base of his spine and shot straight to his balls.

The scent of roses and sex filled the air and he breathed it in.

Her sweet cries surrounded him. He listened and learned, adjusting his thrusts to provide her the greatest pleasure. He straightened and rubbed his thumb against her clit, and with his other hand, he gripped her hip and increased his rhythm just slightly.

Opening her eyes, she bit her bottom lip, and then ran her hands up and down her chest before pinching her nipples. Her mouth opened and her head fell back against the pillow. "Oh yes. Oh, right there, please."

So uninhibited. Fuck, she drove him to madness. He fought against the need to ride her with abandon. No, this moment was for her. Not him.

"Ryan, yes. Yes, I feel it. It's like a wave and it's too much. It's grabbing me."

"Let it happen, baby."

"I am. It's happening...it's squeezing me."

Her hips jerked and her core tightened around his cock. She had a death grip on his arm as she purred out her pleasure with nonsensical words and panted breaths. Then she opened her eyes and met his gaze. So much love was visible within the blue. He lost all control and thrust into her over and over until his back bowed and his balls tightened and then pure pleasure shot out his cock. "Shit." He drew out the word as his hips stuttered against her body.

Still not close enough, he bent and took her mouth, pouring out his love and devotion with messy kisses and deep groans.

Finally, he'd made her his. That caused another shudder to rip through his body and he felt his dick twitch inside her. Insane.

Intense. Complete. Those were the only words he could find to describe this moment.

Once his body stopped shuddering, he collapsed and buried his face in her neck, because okay, maybe a few tears fell, and he didn't want her to question his enjoyment of the experience, plus he was too overwhelmed to explain why he was all teary-eyed anyway.

April in bed. April his. April stay. *Caveman happy.*

On the verge of drifting off, he shifted a little to the side, sure he was suffocating her and figuring he should say something about her first foray into lovemaking.

"Stay, please. Just stay." She locked her arms around him, raking her nails up and down his back.

After a moment, he heard her humming and then she started singing what sounded like Marvin Gaye's, "Ain't No Mountain High Enough."

So of course, he joined in and sang at the top of his lungs, because hell yeah, they'd scaled enough mountains, valleys, and rivers to get right here, right now.

And in this moment, they finally stopped climbing and could revel in sitting at the top of that mountain and shouting to the whole world that they'd made it—together.

CHAPTER 12

April blinked awake, stretching her arms above her head. Her right ear still ached a little and her hip was a bit bruised where she'd landed on the bar's floor, but her other twitches and stings were absolutely glorious. Her body flushed as she thought about what they'd done last night. How soon could they make love again? Maybe now? Yes, now!

Ryan's arm circled her waist and his very hard erection poked her bottom.

Slowly, so as not to wake him, she turned in his arms.

His brown lashes rested against his cheeks. His visage so calm and at ease. His dirty blond hair, a complete mess and smashed to one side. His lips rosy red from their kisses.

A glorious scent filled the air. This must be what sex smelled like, all earthy, thick, and intoxicating. Moaning a little, she crossed her legs together and squeezed. That motion didn't help, only made an intense need fire through her already too-hot system.

She studied Ryan's trim body. A six pack, lightly dusted with hair a shade darker than the light blondish-brown hair on his head. What would he think about her news? She had to tell him soon. Though she hadn't wanted her father's interference in her life, with this one thing, she'd asked—and received. Actually, she'd presented the problem and her father had proceeded to handle everything. Was using her father's influence to get a job fair? She honestly didn't care, because she got to be with Ryan.

Speaking of being with Ryan, his cock was basically waving a very hearty good morning. Perhaps, she'd use this moment to discover what having him in her mouth felt like. She could do this. Be brave. Be bold. He seemed to enjoy her uninhibited expressions of pleasure last night, so why not continue? She *had* declared her desire to stay in bed for days. What better way to prove it?

She slid down his body, tentatively taking his thick cock in her hand. Oh, so smooth, yet hard at the same time.

Ryan shifted onto his back. "April?"

She refrained from giggling then opened her mouth and sucked him into her mouth.

"April!"

"Wha?" Mouth full, she realized he'd never understand her. She grinned a little at that then pulled free. "What?"

"Nothing. Never mind." Ryan lifted the covers and peeked down at her. "Please continue."

She arched a brow. "If you're sure?"

"Oh, I'm sure."

"Because I'm not all that clear on what I'm doing." She gripped his dick again, sliding her hand up and down.

His hips arched a little, and his eyes slid half-closed. "You're doing a fine job."

"Really? How good on a scale of one to ten?"

"April," he growled.

Right? Apparently, he really liked what she was doing, and she'd pushed him a bit too far with her flirtatious questions. Flirtatious? Yes, she smiled, she was definitely flirting. "I'll try to score a ten." Settling between his legs, she bent and slid him deep again then worked her mouth up and down. Gagging a little, she eased off. "I-Is this okay?"

"April, having your mouth on my dick is all I care about.

Touch my balls, my cock, anything you want, I promise anything you do is perfection."

His dick twitched in her hand as if in agreement.

"Very well." She proceeded as requested. He'd certainly done his best to care for her last night, so turnabout was fair play. She even gripped his fuzzy balls in her hand and squeezed, which elicited a gasp so she did it again. Using her other hand, she held his cock steady at the base and bobbed her head up and down until fluid leaked from his tip. Curious, she licked it. Salty and a bit bitter. Still, he'd hissed at her bold action, so she licked him again. This time with the flat of her tongue. She was the one moaning now, and though she wanted to please him this way, her core was aching to be filled.

"Take all of me. Suck hard." Ryan placed a hand on her head and threaded his fingers through her hair.

Taking his cock deep, she sucked in her cheeks then ran her tongue along his base as she came back to the tip.

"Oh, April…fuck, that's amazing."

His words shot like flames straight to her core. Before meeting him, she'd never have dared to think of touching a man this way, but he'd changed her. Made her need and want more, so much more.

"That's good, April." He gentled his grip, directing her with slight up and down pressure.

After a few more passes with her lips, she moaned against his cock as curse words and sharp gasps poured from his lips.

"I'm gonna come. If you don't want to taste me then pull back."

Taste him? Why not? She'd already had a small sample and the flavor was all-Ryan. If she was trying new things, then she wanted to experience everything. In answer to his slight tug on her hair, she sucked on his tip, breathing through her nose.

His hips jerked and hot liquid spurted into her mouth.

She gagged a little but managed to swallow some down.

He eased her away and grabbed his dick, pumping furiously.

She watched mesmerized as a creamy liquid poured from his slit. Then she leaned forward and lapped it up with her tongue.

"April...fuck me." Ryan's entire body shuddered and he pulled his hand from his softening cock. "Come here."

Biting her bottom lip, she slid up his body. "Did you enjoy—"

He tossed her onto her back and rose above her.

She shrieked, but then lost all air as he kissed her hard.

His slightly damp dick brushed against her leg, and she moaned into his mouth.

Tearing away, she tugged on his hip. "I want you inside me again." She tilted her head to the side as he kissed her neck, and then he bent and sucked one nipple into his mouth.

She gasped and lifted her hips against him. "Please...I want more."

He rose above her again and devoured her mouth, stroking deep with his tongue.

Not soft. Not gentle. Wild and out of control, and she loved it.

Scraping her nails down his back, she licked her lips. She could still taste him on her tongue, and the thought that he could taste himself too, drove her mad with desire. Not too long ago she'd have escaped and washed off all their shared germs, but not anymore. Now she wanted to absorb and taste everything...over and over until she was covered and marked and dirty with sex and sweat.

Easing back from his feral kiss, she placed his rejuvenated cock at her center. "Inside me. Now."

"April." Ryan kissed her shoulder. "It's too soon. You'll be sore."

Was he serious? Did he know how sore she was without him inside her? She was throbbing with need. "I don't care."

He growled. "I want to fuck you so hard. I want to pound

you into this mattress until I'm so deep inside you nothing will ever come between us again."

"Then do it." She dug her nails into his butt cheeks. "Fuck me."

"Oh, April." His entire body shivered. "You can't talk like that. My cock will explode." He shook his head. "I don't want to hurt you."

"But I do hurt. I ache to have you inside me. You'll be gentle. I know it." She pulled his lips down to hers and kissed him. "Please."

"Obviously, I'm incapable of saying no to you." Shaking his head, he grabbed another condom from the side table and rose above her once more. "Tell me if this stings and I'll stop."

Slowly, far too slowly for her screaming nerves, he worked his cock into her wet, slightly tender core. Not that she'd ever admit that, because a wash of pleasure flowed through her body. She was his. All his. Twice his. And the entire situation was unabashedly erotic.

"You okay?"

In answer, she gripped his hips and tugged.

"Slow, April," he gritted out between clenched teeth.

"Sorry, but I need more." Relaxing back onto the pillow, she trailed her hands up her body and over her nipples, sensations shot to her core and she gasped.

"Oh, hell…April, that's so fucking hot." Ryan's gaze dropped to watch her movements and his thrusts increased pace. "Don't stop. Keep touching yourself."

He'd seemed a little surprised and his eyes had gone slightly dark when she'd touched her nipples last night, but it felt so good. Maybe other women didn't do this, but she didn't care. She lifted her hips to meet each long slow grind, pinching her nipples and flicking the tips. So much. Too much.

"How about a little more stimulation?" Chest heaving, he lifted her legs onto his shoulders and rubbed against her clit with his thumb.

A spasm shot through her, and she jerked. "Ryan, that's so good. Press harder. Yes, right there. Oh, that's amazing." His finger hit that perfect spot that pinged pleasure throughout her body. His hips rolling his thick cock into her body, his fingers bringing exquisite bliss to her silky wet folds, so close…she fisted her hands in the sheets.

He bent and sucked one nipple into his mouth and that bit of stimulation was all it took.

Her body went rigid and then the waves of ecstasy broke and flowed like pulsing madness though her core and exploded out from there. His thumb kept working on the outside as he plunged inside. And the intensity had her screaming and then biting her hand.

Seemingly wanting to drive her to insane, he bent and kissed her, deeply, driving his tongue into her mouth without rhyme or reason, but then he eased back and gripped her hips. "Look at me, April. Who fucking owns you?"

A pleasurable ping fired through her lower body again, building. Something so intense but just out of reach.

"Who, damn it?"

"You. Only you."

Pounding into her, sweat trickled down the side of his face, his nostrils flared, and he dropped his head back on his shoulders as gasps poured from his lips.

Sensations climbed once more.

"Look at me when you come again. Look at me as I fuck out everything. The past, the pain, the years apart. You are mine, April David. After you come, I'm gonna pull out and mark you with my seed. Hot and fucking wet all over that pristine skin. I'm gonna dirty you up."

"Yes, oh, please. Do it." Her core clamped onto him once more, and she burst with a second orgasm even stronger than the first. She arched off the bed and her guttural scream turned her throat raw as she shuddered again and again.

"Look at me."

Wearily, she opened her eyes as she practically floated in another reality where pleasure ruled and her body remained lost to bliss.

His gaze locked on hers, and he pressed a hand against her chest. Gritting his teeth, he slammed into her core once, twice, and then with a harsh grunt, he pulled his cock free.

She cried at the loss.

Bent on one knee, he eased higher up her body, tugged off the condom, and then pumped his dick until he threw back his head and roared.

Hot cum splattered onto her chest.

She swiped her fingers through the creamy liquid and rubbed it across her nipples.

"Yeah, spread me all over your body." Ryan looked down at her and licked his lips. "Mark that skin."

Pure need shot to her core once more and even though she'd just come twice, she wanted him again. Her entire body felt owned and, in a way, reborn. Slicking her fingers through his seed, she gazed up at him, body flushed, chest heaving. "I want you again. Inside me. I need you there."

After catching his breath, he dropped beside her and brushed her hair behind her ear. "April David, I love you more than life, but my dick needs about twenty minutes."

She slid on top of him. "I can do twenty."

"Wait." He held her by the shoulders so they didn't touch. "Do you need to take a shower?"

"Eventually yes." She smiled down at him. "But I like knowing a part of you is on my skin and I…" She shook her head, slightly unsure if she should admit this fantasy.

"What?" He tipped up her chin. "Don't go all shy on me now."

"I want to feel you inside me without any barriers. I want to feel the heat when you come." She trailed a finger across the cum still drying on her chest. "I know using condoms is necessary for now, but I'll go on the pill right away. Then we can be bare." She shivered. "So bare."

He pressed her onto her back and buried his face in her hair, resting his head against her shoulder. "I absolutely want that."

"Ryan."

"Yeah."

"It took me a while and I'm sorry for that, but I'm happier in this moment than I've ever been in my life. I know we have some adjusting to do and some talking about the future, but I love you and I'm ready."

"I'm ready, too."

As he shook his head, she felt his hair ruffle against her cheek. "Can we just lay here for a while?"

"Absolutely."

She quirked a grin and trailed her fingernails up and down his arm. "Then can we see if you really need twenty minutes?"

Ryan barked out a laugh and settled his thigh over hers. "April David. What am I to do with you?"

Turning to face him, she frowned. "I believe I said what I wanted you to do."

He pressed his lips together. "That you did." Smiling, he tickled her sides until she couldn't breathe. Then he kissed her softly, reverently, until all she could feel was his absolute love for her.

Masterfully using his hands and mouth, he once again drove her body to the pinnacle of pleasure, and now sated, she drifted off to sleep on heart-shaped clouds and rainbow-colored kisses.

#

Fresh from a shared shower, April clutched her towel against her chest and plopped onto Ryan's messy bed. The only clothes she had were from the bar, in a hospital bag, and covered in blood—her blood. Some things were just gross no matter the phobia. She'd likely throw away those clothes, which was irritating because she really liked her Hulk shirt. She sighed. "I need to go back to the hotel."

Ryan stopped scrubbing the towel over his hair.

She stared at his chest. At his abs. At the trail of hair that led to the one thing that could make her cry out in pleasure. The familiar stirring built. Apparently, she couldn't get enough of him. Even now she wanted to feel him moving inside her. Perhaps she'd waited too long to claim him, especially now that she understood how wonderful sex could be. But, she was hungry. Needed clothes.

But then Ryan bent and dried off his leg, and his bits dangled in front of her. *Food? Clothing?* No. She'd rather be naked. In bed. With Ryan. With his bits inside her bits. However, she *was* a little sore. She wouldn't let him know that though.

Ryan ambled over to his dresser, grabbed a T-shirt from a drawer, and tossed it to her. "Put this on for now. We'll go grab your clothes. You're not staying at that hotel anymore, so while we're there you can check out. How long are you here for anyway?"

She tiptoed over to him and placed a hand against his scruffy cheek. "As long as it takes."

"Well, obviously, *it* didn't take long." He placed both hands on her hips and bumped against her.

"You will likely continue to argue that it did."

"I could." He bent and trailed kisses along her neck. "I could torture you until you waited on the edge, just like I did for three years."

April drew in sharp breath as pleasure zipped through her body.

He tugged on the front of her towel.

She wiggled and let it fall to the floor.

He stepped back, grinning then lifted a hand. "No. No. Not again. Food then hotel."

"Oh, I know you're hungry." She ran a finger down his chest. "For me."

Smiling, he gripped her wayward hand before she could entice him further. Then he picked up the towel and placed it back around her body. "April, I want you more than anything, but you're…new to this, and I won't hurt you."

"Okay." Maybe by tonight she'd be less sore. The sting and slight ache would fade. Not that they couldn't do other things. She was sure Ryan knew of many, many things. She shivered then pulled him close for a kiss, which quickly got out of hand and her towel fell to the floor again.

"No." He eased back, hands lifted at his sides. "Food and hotel. Food and hotel."

April sighed. "Yes, food and hotel."

He gave her a once over. "You are the most beautiful thing I've ever seen."

"Thank you." Her cheeks heated and she clutched her hands together at her waist. "I enjoy your body, too."

"Enjoy?" He huffed out a laugh. "I'm not hot? Handsome? Sexier than shit?"

"Well you are…sexier than…um…shit."

He burst out laughing. "Get dressed, pottymouth. We'll feed you and get your things so you're back here where you belong."

"Speaking of where I belong, I need to tell you something."

CHAPTER 13

After hearing April's tone, Ryan stilled with his boxer briefs in hand. He quickly tugged them on. Wow. Her tone was very serious...almost fearful. This should be interesting. Maybe they *should* go back to making love. Those moments with her were embedded in his brain and heart forever. So amazing. Before he could get sidetracked with those thoughts, he pressed a hand against his thickening cock and faced April. "Do you want to tell me now or while we're eating?" He grabbed black gym shorts from another drawer and pulled them on.

"I'd like to tell you now." She pulled his T-shirt over her body. "Do you have food here?"

"No, but I could order something."

"Yes, I could eat pizza." She nodded decisively.

"Well I do live in a college town. I can get something besides pizza. What about Indian food?"

Her pert nose scrunched up. "I like pizza."

He chuckled then stopped when he caught sight of her legs, spilling out from under his shirt. Bare. She was bare beneath there. A surge of possessiveness, and a whole lot of lust, washed through him. The image did things to him. Everything was finally falling into place. April was staying right here, in his clothes, forever. Well, not literally, but whatever.

He followed her to the kitchen and pulled a couple menus from his catch-all drawer. "What kind of pizza?"

"I'd like a place that has salad and beer."

"Drinking beer and eating pizza kind of negates the whole healthy salad concept. Plus, they won't deliver beer."

April opened his fridge and peered inside. The shirt road up dangerously, baring her legs and hinting at her fine ass.

"Do you think they wash their salads?"

"What?" He shook his head. What was she saying?

"I asked about the salad." She glanced at him with a slight frown. "Never mind. Just order what you'd like."

He grinned. Ms. Phobia wasn't completely cured and honestly knowing that didn't bother him at all. He had a few quirks of his own. He placed a call for pizza, and even ordered a salad, which may or may not get eaten, and then handed April a beer, which she downed immediately before asking for another. She carried her bottle into the living room and plopped on his couch. "I probably shouldn't be drinking alcohol with the pills I'm taking, but I'm thirsty and I don't care."

"Are you thirsty or nervous?" He settled on the couch beside her.

She tilted her head back and forth. "I'm both."

"Okay...why nervous?"

"Well, I have good news." She turned to face him, bending one leg under her bottom. "But I don't know how you'll feel about it due to what's happened in the past."

What happened in the past? Lots of shit had happened, so...he had no idea what she meant. "April, we're both very blunt people, so just spit it out."

She heaved in a deep breath. "I'm your assistant."

"My assistant." Not at all what he expected her to say. Maybe he should drink a couple beers, because, *What?*

She stood and fiddled her fingers together like she used to when she was nervous at the tea shop.

"April, it's okay." He leaned forward and placed a hand over hers.

She frowned. "Habit. I can't seem to stop."

"It's okay. I like it. It's familiar. And it's you. But explain, and don't be worried. I'm listening."

"All right." She met his gaze then nodded. "I went to my father about six months ago and I told him I was ready to see you. I'd been thinking a lot about what I wanted to do. You know I've been taking law classes too, yes?"

"Yes."

"Well, I've done well with my studies, and I'm almost finished. I know how hard Father works, and I know how hard you'll work. It's in your nature to do so, and you'll want to prove yourself in your new job. I understand this."

"Yes, you know I'm working for York and Graff."

"Actually that's what started my…worries. You see, I want to be with you. And maybe this is too much, but I want to be with you all the time. I've wasted…well, not wasted, but I've been apart from you for too long. And you see, your new job…based on my father's work hours, I knew I'd continue to be apart from you, so I fixed it."

"Fixed it how?" He had a sinking sensation in his stomach. David machinations were at play here, but to what end?

"I asked my father to help me get a job." She bit her bottom lip. "Uh…with you."

"With me?"

"Yes…as your, uh…assistant."

"What?" He raked his fingers through his hair. Still feeling like a puppet on the David family strings.

"I'm sorry."

"No, April. You're not." Frowning, he met her gaze. "Are there no bounds to the David manipulations? I wanted to get this job on my own."

She dropped to her knees before him and took his hands.

"Oh, Ryan, you did."

"No." He pulled away his hands and slouched back against the couch. "Your *father* secured me a position. Again. Do you know how that makes me feel? I worked really hard for three years. I earned that job, no one should give it to me."

April narrowed her eyes and huffed out a breath. "I just said, I did *not* get my job until after you did, and I promise you no one knows of our relationship, because when the request was made, we didn't really have one, did we?"

Choosing not to argue the fact that they did, in fact, have a relationship, he focused more on this David family maneuvering of chess pieces. Ryan clenched his jaw and rubbed his temple. "People will wonder if your dad got me the job."

"When have you ever cared about what people think?"

He grunted.

"I'm not sorry." April stood again, hands braced on her hips. "I *will* work hard for you I promise. You won't regret having me as your assistant. I'm very intelligent, and I've spent the past three years mirroring your studies."

"Is that so?"

"Yes, actually I could do your job quite easily."

"Modest much?"

"No."

"So, you've planned it all out, have you?" He stared at the blonde beauty before him. She'd always surprised him, so this was actually just par for the course.

"Yes. I believe I planned things quite satisfactorily."

"Didn't even ask if you could come to Maine, just insinuated yourself in my life and even my job." Brows lifted high, he stared at her, waiting to hear her argument.

"Yes." Her imperious David-chin lifted. "I won't lose you. I will go with you, and we'll work together. We are a team whether you like it or not."

"Obviously it doesn't matter if *I* like it or not," he drawled.

"It's done." Although she was correct in that, she would likely have spent little time with him as he'd settled into his job. *Damn it!* She was right. Her plan was solid, made sense, and would work. But he was supposed to be securing their future, and he hadn't even considered this huge issue.

"Are you truly upset?"

The answer to that question was still a resounding *yes*, but he was softening to the idea. "What's your title?"

"I'm a paralegal."

"And you work for me?" Oh, this could get naughty, very fast. April in skirts. April bending over to pick up a dropped pen. April in his office late at night. Okay, so maybe this *was* a good idea.

"Yes. I will assist you by filing documents, record keeping, research, and litigation support. You'll have a separate receptionist, as well."

"And you're willing to work long hours?"

"Of course."

"You're willing to do whatever I ask?"

"Yes."

Grabbing her arm, he tossed her onto the couch, and then rose above her. "You're willing to bend over my desk and lift your skirt any time I ask?"

She sucked in a breath. "Would you ask that of me?"

"Absolutely."

"I think those sorts of behaviors are against company policy, Ryan."

"No. You're mine. And I'll be rewriting your job description to suit my needs."

"You're angry." She pressed a finger between his brows.

"Yes."

"You're bullying me to show your displeasure."

"Oh, I'll be showing you my displeasure in *our* office as often as possible."

"Hmm…I hadn't thought of that."

"Really?" He kissed her neck and licked the shell of her ear.

"No, but now that we've…um…had sex…I can understand why you'd be interested."

"April."

"Yes." Her word was practically a pant.

"You and your father need to stop controlling my life." Narrowing his eyes, he eased back, bracing a hand on the back of the couch. "Talk to me before you do something like that again."

She bit her bottom lip. "I only want to be with you."

"And I with you."

"Then I don't understand why you're upset."

"Yes, you do."

"Okay." She dropped her gaze. "I do, but I want us to work together. If we didn't then I'd never see you."

He hummed out his agreement. "I hadn't thought that far ahead."

"Well… I did." She sniffed. "I told you I'm very smart."

"Smart or a manipulator like your father?"

"He wants me to be happy. Being with you and working a job I've studied very hard for will make me happy. I was lucky to get this job. I did have to interview, you know." She crossed both arms over her chest and shot him a glare.

"Ha! I'm surprised they didn't want to have you as their assistant." He envisioned her gorgeous self walking into that office and all the jaws dropping. "They probably took one look at you and became hypnotized by your beauty."

April cleared her throat and looked away.

"Oh shit. I'm right, aren't I?"

"The job was for *your* assistant, so I explained that I only wanted to work for you. Actually…well…um, my father told him."

"April." He shifted so he sat on the couch and held her in his arms. "What happened?"

She gripped his hand and played with his fingers. "Well, the man I interviewed with…"

"What was his name?"

"Michael Baldwin."

Ah, hell, he was the main partner's uncle.

"He said two positions were open, and I said I only wanted the one with Ryan Cole, because I felt we could learn together. He offered me more money to work with him, and I said no and left."

"And then what?"

"He called an offered me the job to work with you."

"*After* he spoke to your father, no doubt." Ryan dropped his head back against the couch, groaning.

"Stop that." She rolled her eyes. "I spoke to Father about my trip to Maine, and if he called the man after we spoke, I don't truly know."

"Fucking hell, April." He rested his forearm across his eyes.

"Quit being so ridiculous." She heaved a sigh and pulled away his arm. "It's not bad to have a United States senator with aspirations to the presidency on your side, Ryan. Goodness gracious, calm down."

"You interviewed for a job *with me*, didn't see fit to tell me, and then your father secures your position." He scoffed. "Don't tell me to calm down, because having your father's influence won't always work in my favor. Politics can be a touchy thing, April."

"Mr. Baldwin is friends with Father from back in their college days."

Ryan sighed. "I'll have to work harder now."

"And you think I won't?" April's head shot up, her hair brushing against his face. "Everyone will know my father got me the job, because essentially he did, but I am skilled. I ask that you give me a chance."

"You want to work as a team?" He pinched her chin between his forefinger and thumb.

"Yes, please." She licked her lips and then climbed onto his lap, kissing him. Well…placating him…but he'd take it.

He wrapped his arms around her, angled his head, and kissed her with passion and a slight edge of anger. After last night, his sexual appetites were hardly slaked. He wanted more. With each dive of his tongue, he made clear how much he wanted her. Conveyed who was in charge. Because, at least here, he was the master. Soon, she'd become the skilled student, and Lord, help him then.

Teasing her with barely-there kisses, he pressed her back onto the couch.

The doorbell rang.

"Damn, that's shitty timing." He laughed and shifted his cock in his shorts. "Food and hotel." Actually, the pizza arriving *was* good timing, because if not, he'd have taken her again. Some sort of reassertion of dominance thing. Which wasn't right. But would have felt so fucking good.

"Ryan." April piped up from the couch.

He glanced over his shoulder. Her lips were red. Her hair a fluffed mess. Her eyes slightly hooded.

"Why don't you let your assistant get that?"

He watched as her slender fingers took cash from his wallet on the kitchen counter, and remained mesmerized as her long legs walked to the door.

All right, he'd admit, he could get used to watching her all day. He sighed. *A team, huh?* He could do that. He wouldn't tell her he was pleased with her machinations. Not for a while. They'd have to set some ground rules but having her with him *would* work. She was smart, and had a fantastic memory.

Wait a minute, long legs? She was still in his T-shirt. Only, his T-shirt. He rushed to the door and shoved her away from the ogling pizza delivery boy.

"Hold on a sec, Ms. Paralegal." He jerked his head toward the kitchen. "Go get your boss a drink."

The pizza guy was wide-eyed with his jaw slightly open when Ryan faced him again.

"Um…sorry, but she's…like wow."

Ryan could only nod. "You have no idea."

# # #

In Ryan's T-shirt and a pair of his old sweats, April hummed along with the car radio as they headed to the hotel.

Her guess-what-I'm-your-new-assistant reveal had gone about as well as she'd figured. Cheri had warned her about Ryan's male pride and how he wouldn't like her working behind his back. She'd even reminded April how the last time her father had interfered with their relationship it'd kept them apart for three years. To which, April agreed to an extent, but at the same time, their separation was something she'd chosen.

Once Ryan started working at York and Graff, he'd be fresh on the job, trying to prove his worth. Working long hours. Preoccupied. So, she'd manipulated her way closer to him. Found a way to be a part of his new life. Plus, she *had* always dreamed of a career as a lawyer. Just like her father. However, due to her somewhat dicey background, she'd likely never get hired, so she'd settle for a job as paralegal with a boss named Ryan Cole. Together they'd be the best team ever. She just knew it. She also hoped to continue her counseling work in Maine. Since Ryan's focus was Family Law, she was sure she'd have plenty of opportunities. Considering that, she'd have to schedule time with Britni again soon.

She glanced over at her future boss, sitting in the driver's seat. She wanted him again. Would this craving ever stop? Ever since he'd told her he'd have sex with her on his work desk, those images, along with a few even naughtier ones, played like a bad porno in her mind. Groaning, she squirmed in her seat.

"Keep making noises like that, and I'll stop this car and fuck you in the backseat."

"You say that as if I don't want it to happen. Can we?" She glanced around at the busy streets. Hmmm…maybe a side road led to someplace more discreet.

"No, although I'm tempted."

"What about when we get to my hotel room?"

"April…I don't know how to be delicate about this, but are you feeling okay…you know, there?"

She felt her cheeks heat so she glanced out the side window. "Yes."

"You're lying. Don't lie."

"Okay, no, but I don't care."

He took her hand. "I do. Stop directing things. It's okay. We're okay. I'm not going anywhere."

April pulled free from his grip and ran her damp palms along her loaned sweatpants. "I spent so long having no control, and now that I have some, I want things to go my way." She frowned. "I've decided I'm a selfish person."

"Hell, we're all selfish." Ryan flicked on the turn signal to exit to her hotel. "Don't let anyone tell you any different."

"*You're* not."

A few more blocks and they pulled into the Charles Hotel parking garage. With only two levels, he had to circle around for a minute to find an empty spot.

After parking, he turned in the seat and faced her. "Yeah, April. I am very selfish."

"In what way?"

"In every way. First and foremost, I'm not willing to share you with anyone. I want to grab your things, take you back to my place, and hide you there until we have to leave."

"I want that too though, so it's not really selfish."

He grabbed her hand. "I suppose. Plus, it'll be good to take some time now that we've cooled our more animalistic urges. We can talk and get familiar with each other again. Find a level of comfort between us. Sure, we've talked and texted, but in person everything's kind of different. Having you here is real and it's raw and it's so very right, but we've never lived together, or worked together, so bumps will happen, babe."

"I agree." His words made absolute sense. Talking on the phone was like looking at pictures in a photo album. Only happy moments were highlighted. Day-to-day struggles weren't captured. They'd both have to make adjustments, but she didn't doubt they'd have more good days than bad. "Shall we go on dates? Is that a good idea? I've been asked out by men, quite a bit actually."

"What?" Ryan snapped around to face her. "What do you mean, you've been asked out? By who?"

"I explained that I've been socializing with Dewey and Maria. While I am out, I'm frequently approached by men who talk to me and ask me out. I even had a man speak to me at the teashop a few times. He was actually very attractive. He had blond hair like yours and…"

"No." Ryan growled and shook his head.

"No?"

"We are *not* discussing this."

April frowned. "But Ryan, I didn't date any of them."

He ripped the keys from the ignition and grabbed his cell from the cup holder. "Get out of the car, April."

"You're so bossy." She narrowed her eyes. "I'm sure women have been interested in you, too. Your Shelby for example, and you *do* work as a bartender. Maria says all women love a bartender."

He shrugged and grinned. "Yeah, they do."

April had visions of dumping tip jars on flirtatious women's heads.

"See." He poked her ribs. "Not a fun discussion."

"I will concede your point." She sniffed.

"Come on. Let's get your things." He jerked his head toward

the elevators. "We have plenty of time to talk about everything."

After he opened her car door, she took his hand. Cool early-fall air hit her cheeks. She sidestepped to avoid a bit of gum on the pavement. "So, you didn't answer the question. Would you like to date me, Ryan?"

"April, I think we're past that." He squeezed her hand.

"Well, I liked it when we went to the movies before, and you cooked me dinner, and we had cupcakes…remember the cupcakes?"

"Yes, I remember your plethora of cakes."

"Plethora?" She arched a brow.

"I did just graduate from Harvard."

"Hmmm…"

He chuckled then tugged her into the garage's elevator and pressed the button for the lobby. "What's your room number?"

"I'm in the Dean's Suite"

"Okay. Top floor?"

"Well, Father has the Presidential Suite."

"Right, yes, nothing but the best for Senator David."

After riding up the elevator, they exited into the lobby.

"The elevators to the room's are over here." Taking his hand, April led him through the typical lobby set-up of couches, tables, and fake plants. Once in the elevator, she used her special keycard to gain access to her floor. They shot up and then the elevator shuddered to a stop. She steered Ryan to her room, still not convinced they couldn't have sex once inside. Just outside her room's door, she peeked at him, considering the best way to proceed.

His gaze was locked on his phone.

"Ryan?"

"Sorry, I was reading a text from Shelby." He raked his fingers through his hair. "She's sent like ten texts."

His phone rang with some hip-hop song's ring tone.

He glanced at April then back to his phone. "I'm sorry, but I feel like I should take this. It's Shelby."

"All right." Conflicting emotions flashed through April's mind. Jealousy. Anger. Sympathy. And more jealousy. Plus, her ear still *did* hurt. "I know Shelby is your friend."

"Was. She *was* my friend."

"She is." Dropping her gaze, April nodded toward his phone. "I'll leave the door open for you. Come in when you're ready."

She watched him walk back down the hall toward the elevators, his posture very tense and his tone terse.

What would Shelby say in her defense? April did feel a tad bit of sympathy for the woman. She was obviously in love with Ryan, and not having those feelings returned would hurt. "You and Ryan have enough issues of your own, April David. You need to focus on those…and places we could go on a date. I can be more creative than a movie for goodness sakes." Sighing, she stepped into the bedroom then rolled her bright-blue suitcase out of the closet.

Humming an old Celine Dion tune about the heart going on and on, she packed away her toiletries in her polka dot bag.

Footsteps shuffled across the carpet.

A floorboard creaked.

She could do this. Ask how Shelby was doing. Not be so jealous. Inhaling deeply, April glanced into the bathroom mirror. "I'm almost finished. How is—"

Dr. Ashburn stood behind her.

Bloodshot eyes.

Rumpled shirt.

A glint of silver in his hand.

The tip of a corkscrew pressed against her neck.

Her vein bulged as blood rushed through her system.

He met her gaze in the mirror. "Just where do you think you're going?"

CHAPTER 14

An unholy scream ripped down the hallway.

Ryan stilled with his cell plastered against his ear. Had that come from April?

April!

"What was that?" Shelby shouted through the phone.

"I gotta go." Heart racing, Ryan bolted down the hallway.

April's door was wide open.

Voices came from further within.

Though every muscle in his body wanted to sprint to her rescue, he crept closer to the bedroom and peered into the bathroom.

He saw them in the mirror.

April in Ashburn's arms.

Her eyes wide. Her jaw set.

Why was he holding her like that?

Why had she screamed?

Was that blood trickling down her neck?

Fuck caution, his woman was bleeding.

He shot forward. "What the fuck are you doing?"

"She's coming with me." Ashburn glared, keeping April in his arms. He backed up against the bathroom door, dragging her along with him.

"You're kidnapping her with a corkscrew?" Ryan shook his head. Everything in him wanted to leap to April's rescue. He wanted to beat Ashburn until the man was bloody at his feet. "Have you lost your mind?"

"Get out of my way." Ashburn continued to shuffle along the door, pulling April with him. "She doesn't belong with you. She's mine."

April's gaze was locked on the arm holding the corkscrew. Was she recalling her captivity? Would this push her back into her shell?

"Why are you doing this?" Ryan shouted. "You're versed in avoiding these kinds of psychotic-behaviors, so what the hell are you doing?" Had the guy been taking too many of his own meds? Ryan drew in a deep breath and slowly let it out, keeping his gaze on Ashburn the whole time. "Listen, I get that you care for her. She's a lovely woman. I understand the attachment."

"You understand nothing." Ashburn eased another step out of the bathroom.

"Maybe not." Feigning compliance, he lifted both hands, palms up. "But *April* understands. She cares about you. And right now you're scaring her. Don't do this. She's come so far and she trusts you. Please, drop the wine opener. Please."

"I'll drop it if you let me leave."

"I'm sorry." Ryan tried to keep his tone smooth when pure rage was firing through his system. "I can't do that. Let's all take a big breath, and we'll sit in the living room and talk this through, all right?"

"No. Nothing is all right." Ashburn's nostrils flared as he dragged April along the bedroom wall, trying to side-step him. "We were fine until you came along. You ruined everything."

"I know." Ryan glanced at April. She looked…calculating. *Oh, hell no.* "I will likely ruin everything, but if you don't give April and me a chance, she'll resent you forever."

Ashburn blinked.

"You're smarter than this." Could he tackle the guy without injuring April? He'd wait for the perfect opening. He kept his tone calm as he placated the man. "You're also right about April and I. We don't suit, and she'll discover that in time." The words were like acid on his tongue, especially when April gasped and her gaze bored into him. He avoided her narrowed eyes and focused on Ashburn. "Drop the corkscrew. Let her go or she'll never forgive you."

Ashburn glanced down at her. "I would never hurt you."

"Is that so? Well, I can't say the same." April grabbed Ashburn's arm and sort of shrugged.

The next thing Ryan knew, she'd stepped to the side, turned her body, hauled back and slapped Ashburn's ear. Then she screamed like a wild banshee and kneed the son of a bitch in the nuts.

Ashburn grunted and dropped to his knees.

Chest heaving, April kicked Ashburn's side again and again while profanities poured from her sweet lips.

Holy shit!

"April. Stop!" Ryan rushed to her side and pulled her away from her unconscious therapist.

She fought him off, screaming and thrashing.

"Baby, it's me. Stop. Stop." Ryan held her tight. "Stop fighting."

He caught a glint of silver out of the corner of his eye.

The corkscrew had landed on the carpet.

For a moment, a red haze fell over him and he wanted nothing more than to pick up the weapon and thrust it through Ashburn's heart.

Furious, Ryan kicked the corkscrew across the room.

April whimpered.

"It's okay." Her body shook as if she was in a paint can mixer, and her fingers dug like claws into his back. "Let me see." He tilted her face to the side. "Are you okay?"

"Mmpff." She nodded but didn't lift her head from where it was buried in his chest.

He couldn't look over at the crumpled form of Ashburn without raging, so he drew April into the living room, away from the violence and the betrayal of someone she had cared and trusted most of her life. "We'll call the police. They'll take him away. You were so brave." He kissed her forehead. "My brave, brave, April."

"Ryan." Her voice was barely above a whisper and tears streamed down her cheeks. "W-we need to c-call my...my f-father." Her hand wiped at the blood on her neck. She held it in front of her face and sort of wilted in his arms.

"No. Don't break now. You just kicked Ashburn's ass, so stay with me." He tugged her hand away from her face and led her back to the bathroom. Maybe not so smart as Ashburn was still on the floor, but she was on the verge of freaking out, and so was he. "Here, wash off the blood."

"But...but...the corkscrew...it's dirty. It's probably dirty."

"Then, we'll find some Neosporin for your neck. It's okay. I'm sure it's never been used before." With a shaky hand, he pulled her hair away from her neck. Just a slight scratch. Not too deep. "You're fine. It'll only need a tiny Band-Aid." He wasn't sure who he was trying to convince. And he still wanted to kick Ashburn in the head. Gritting his jaw, he pulled his phone from his pocket and dialed Dewey, because that dude would get shit done.

Dewey answered on the second ring. "What?"

"I need you and Senator David in April's room. Now."

"What's happened?"

"Ashburn."

Dewey grunted out a curse. "On my way."

Ryan tried ignoring the specks of red on the white washcloth. He closed his eyes and breathed through his mouth so the copper scent wouldn't create some kind of animal chaos where he'd lose his mind and fuck up the man still unconscious outside the bathroom door. Just one punch, he'd love just one. Please fucker, just flicker an eyelid and then he could hit him, just once.

April shivered and he caught her looking at Ashburn. "Don't look at him. Dewey and your father are on their way. They'll take care of...things."

Seeing the man on the floor in a fetal position, Ryan couldn't stop the unwelcome wave of sympathy crashing through his mind. If he lost April, he'd probably be in the same position. But he hadn't—and wouldn't—lose her.

A wobbly voice came from the woman pressed against his chest. "I used my self-defense moves, Ryan. I did it."

"I know. I'm proud of you."

"I'm really independent, aren't I?"

He peered into her eyes. "Yes, independent, brave, strong, beautiful. Everything I need in a woman and more."

"My self-defense instructor told me to be confident I could control the situation, and I let that thought consume me before I made my move. I never believed it would work, but I grabbed his arm and did my spin move and..."

Ryan let April ramble on and on, because he understood this was how she processed things that scared her. Fidgeting, rambling, and yeah, kicking ass. That was his April. He soothed her with kisses on her cheeks and brushed his fingers through her hair as he listened to her and found his own calm. She was stronger now. She could fight her own demons. But he'd still keep his arms around her. He'd always be in her corner as an encourager, support system, and best friend.

April kept up the one-sided dialogue until Dewey and her father barreled through the door. And though, Ryan had chafed at the Senator fixing situations in the past, he had to agree that having him handle Ashburn, while he kept April occupied was the perfect solution for everyone. He'd learned a few things over the past three years, too.

He could rely on people, and he kind of liked having a family, even if it wasn't his own. Family rallied around one another during tough times. He hadn't experienced that support system as a child, but he had it now. And he couldn't be more grateful. For the Senator. For Dewey. And for April.

CHAPTER 15

On the couch in her hotel room, April held Cheri's hand as Ryan conferred with her father. Cheri had gone down to the front desk and asked for a first aid kit so April's neck was disinfected and covered in a bandage. Dewey was flying Dr. Ashburn back to Indiana where the therapist would stay in a private facility and get his mind straight.

April was proud she'd defended herself—and Ryan too, in a way. At least that's what she'd told herself, because she *had* hit Ashburn rather hard. And now her hand hurt.

But she wouldn't escape into her prescription drugs that numbed her feelings. She would handle this mix of emotions and process everything in time. But today, and in the immediate future, all she wanted to focus on was her future with Ryan.

She'd never asked for Ashburn's attentions, and after his behavior tonight, she really didn't want to think about him anymore. She could tell by everyone's worried glances that they believed she'd disappear into nothingness again, and she couldn't blame them, since she'd done so in the past. Yet, bad things happened in life. She had to accept that fact and move on. She would continue to fight for the happy times and for what she wanted. And what she wanted was Ryan.

Her road to understanding that, and unraveling who she

wanted to be hadn't been easy. It'd been fraught with self-doubt and fear, plus phobias she even now fought to contain, but she was here now. Ready to fight. Ready for all her plans and dreams to fall into place. Would everything be simple and easy? No. This, she understood. She still had a lot to learn about Ryan and he had a lot to learn about her. Little things. Couple things. Intimate things. Maybe naughty things, too. Yes, those should definitely come first.

With those thoughts in her head, she eased away from Cheri. "I'm really fine, you know. I'd like to rest now, please." Rest with Ryan in her bed, and then food, and then more Ryan. She stifled a giggle. She'd almost been stabbed to death and she was only thinking about sex. But wasn't sex primal? Wasn't almost dying a good time to rejoice in everything she had?

Cheri patted her hand. "Are you sure?"

"Yes. I'm very sure."

Ready for everyone to leave, April stood and walked over to Ryan and her father. She wrapped her dad in a hug. "Thank you for handling Dr. Ashburn discretely. I believe he is confused. And maybe, lonely."

"We shall see." Her father's gaze narrowed onto her neck and he frowned. "Don't you worry about him. I will see to his care."

"Thank you. If I need to find another psychiatrist in Maine, I will. I'll research the best options as I feel I do need to continue my sessions. I'll be making a lot of changes in the coming months." She turned to Ryan and smiled. "Changes I'm more than ready for, but I must remember, I need a little help sometimes."

Ryan wrapped an arm around her waist and kissed her temple. "I'll be beside you, whatever you may need."

Cheri came to her father's side. "Paul, let's leave them be."

"Oh…yes, of course. Have a good night and be sure the door is shut and locked."

April hugged him again. "I will, Father." Then she hugged Cheri. "I'll check in later."

Cheri eased back and nodded. "Get some rest." She winked and led her father to the door.

Her father stopped and glanced over his shoulder. "I'm so glad you're safe…and that you're well again." He nodded at Ryan. "Take care of my girl."

"I will."

He smiled and led Cheri out the door.

April faced Ryan. "I can take care of you too, you know."

"I know you can."

"Do you?" She hoped he was proud of her now. That he could see how much she'd changed.

"Yes." He cupped her face before kissing her.

A soft kiss, full of reverence and love. On and on, it drew out, but didn't turn into anything more. Just a kiss two people in love could share. A slanting of heads. A crossing of tongues. A reminder that they belonged in each other's arms. A glorious moment. A forever memory.

This was what she'd fought three years to find. A home and comfort and Ryan.

She eased back. "I've dreamed of this moment. When I could love you as you deserved. When I could give you my heart completely. It's whole now, and it's all yours."

"Thank you for that gift." He kissed her again. Just a soft press of his lips against hers before he wrapped her in his arms. "*My* heart's still thumping like mad. I'm full of adrenaline, and anger, and rage, and so much confusion over how that all went down. I wanted to beat the hell out of the guy, but…at the same time…"

"At the same time?"

Sighing, he brushed her hair over her shoulder before bending and kissing the tip of her right ear. "I understand that you're easy to love but hard to lose. I still don't know how I survived these past three years without you."

"I'm here now." April clutched the front of his shirt in her hands. "Not that I want to ruin the moment, but I-I don't know how I feel about Dr. Ashburn. I feel like he was becoming a fly, buzzing around my head. *In* my head, actually. I wanted to be free of him." She plunked her head against Ryan's chest. "I don't know how to help him."

Lifting her chin, he kissed her hard. Once. Twice. "I was so scared. I saw the blood on your neck, and I wanted to rip him apart, but I also knew he couldn't be handled that way. Not when you were in danger."

"Ryan, you should not worry." She wasn't sure why she had to keep explaining this. "I am very skilled in self-defense. I've taken weekly classes."

He grinned. "Good to know."

"Stop. You're placating me, and I'm tempted to show you what else I can do."

"Oh, I'll let you take me down anytime, April David." He bumped his hips against hers.

She pursed her lips to keep from grinning, because he was just too full of himself sometimes. "I will, Ryan Cole."

"I hope so."

"I'm sure you do." Rolling her eyes, she tugged him over to the couch and shoved him down.

He laughed and pulled her beside him.

Grinning like crazy, she settled against his side and pulled his hand over her shoulder so she could play with his fingers. "Hands are a funny thing. They can bring you pain and pleasure. They can tell a story with just the simplest movement. I want to hold this hand forever. I want it to wear a ring, sealing me to you. I want these fingers to caress my skin. I want you to hold my hand when I need a friend." She turned to face him. "Three years ago, I let you go. Three years ago, I didn't know who I was, but I knew I was hurt. By you. By my father, because you didn't believe in me.

But, I didn't really believe in myself either. I could excuse my behavior by saying, I'd been through so much. Trauma. Pain. Loss. But you've felt those things and you still stood on your own. Strong and defiant. So, for you, I fought and I cried and I screamed sometimes."

"I've always believed in you. I just waited until you believed the same."

She bit her lip, holding back tears. "I love you to madness. I want you like crazy. I need you like Earl Grey. Every day. An addiction. A craving. And I'll love you like that every day, because I fought for you. Because you believed in me. I won't ever take us for granted."

A single tear trickled down his cheek. "You've always been so beautiful both inside and out. I love you the same way. Hard, deep, and forever." He ran his thumb along her bottom lip. "Your father may have manipulated us. But, I'll always be grateful for the day I met him, because it led me to you. I love you, April David."

She grinned, knowing she'd never tire of hearing those words. "I have another secret."

His brows rose. "Is that so?"

Clearing her throat, she gazed at his damp lips then into his eyes before she became too distracted. "I may have already researched places to live in Maine."

Groaning, he shook his head. "Of course you have, you're April David."

She laughed then sobered a bit. "Yes, I am. I *am* April David. I'm the woman who loves you. The woman who escaped her cage for you. And the woman who needs you to be okay with my...my maybe a little domineering ways."

"A little?" He huffed out a laugh.

"So, you're okay with us being roommates?"

"We're roommates? I thought you'd just *researched* places?"

"Um..."

Ryan clasped a hand around the back of her neck and pulled

her in for a soft, sweet kiss. "Three years ago, I wanted to mold you into the right woman *for me*, but you've been perfect all along. So, yes, I'll be your roommate. But there's just a slight problem." He tapped a finger against his lips.

"What's that?" Her heart raced. What was wrong? Did he already have a place?

"I assume…that in this apartment, we'll share a bed?"

"Yes."

"I see." He stood and lifted her from the couch. "Then I think we need to do some field work."

"Field work?"

He paced around her, like a cat circling its prey. "Being in bed together, you know. How's that going to play out? Are you a cover hog? Left or right side?" He stopped and pressed against her side, whispering in her left ear. "How many times I'll need to fuck you before you can sleep at night? How long it takes you to get ready for work after morning sex? Just how loud our headboard can bang against the wall and not disturb the neighbors. We have a lot of research to do."

"I agree." She adopted a very serious face. "Shall we begin?"

"Absolutely."

She released a loud whoop then ran into the bedroom and hopped on the bed.

He followed, moving slowly, seductively. Oh, she was in for it now.

"So, Mr. Cole, just how shall we begin the so-called research?"

He grinned and tossed his shirt on the floor. "At page one until we reach the end."

"There's an end?"

"Multiple endings."

"Oh, I like those." She spread open her arms. "Show me."

He laid down beside her and pressed a soft kiss against her lips. "Before we begin, I want you to know, I'm glad you're here."

For Ryan

"Me, too."

"No. *You* are *here*. All of you. Finally. And I can see it and feel it. You love me as I love you."

"You can see that?"

He ran a finger down her nose. "It's in your eyes. All the fear and doubt is gone."

"I can't hide how I feel."

"I'd never ask you to."

"I'm finally happy."

"That matters."

"It does, yes." She grinned, sort of hating to break up this sweet moment, but a woman had needs, and he'd gone all heavy-eyed and his body was so warm against hers. "You know what matters more?"

"No."

"Research." With a laugh, she shoved him back on the mattress and began a very, very long and thorough study with, as promised, multiple happy endings.

EPILOGUE

Six months later.

Breathing deeply after a round of very intense lovemaking, April tugged the quilted blanket up over her shoulders.

They'd moved in together, worked together, loved and fought together. Adjustments were made and she loved Ryan more with each passing day. So many facets of him existed and she wanted to flush them all out.

They'd taken a three-day weekend and drove to Moose Lake in Northern Maine to stay at a bed and breakfast. Ryan's idea to which she'd happily agreed. While she loved their apartment and her job—and she really loved her sometimes-naughty boss, she liked the idea of escaping together for a time.

Ryan cleared his throat and got up from the bed. "I'll…uh…I'll be back. Just gonna grab a washcloth."

"Okay." She couldn't keep her eyes open and may have drifted off a little until Ryan shoved her shoulder. "What? You put me to sleep then you wake me up. Not fair."

He was sitting on the side of the bed, one leg bent in front of him, totally naked except for the blue box in his hand. "Marry me."

She shot up and gripped his face in both her hands. "Yes."

"That simple." He grinned.

"Yes." She kissed all over his face like crazy until he laughed and held her close. "We're simple, you and I. We're meant to be together. I'll love you forever, and I'm already all yours. I don't need a piece of paper to signify that, but I'll gladly claim you any way you want."

"I believe I just did claim you many times."

She chuckled. "Yes, you did." She sighed and slumped in his arms. "I remember how you used to chastise me at the teashop. *Look at me, April. Answer me, April. You're rude, April.* No one had ever spoken to me like that. You fascinated me. I would go home so angry and frustrated, but I would dream of you, and I kept going back for more. I craved that attention, and I needed someone to startle me out of my funk."

"Not really a funk."

"You scared me when I needed to be scared. You did everything right and now here we are."

"April, look at me."

She rolled her eyes then met his gaze. "I don't know why that bossiness works."

"Because you love me."

"Yeah, I do. Now, put that ring on my finger and kiss me."

And he kissed her then and every other time she asked. On their wedding day, during their move into their first house, the day of his promotion, and the day they both decided they wanted to stop working so hard and joined a small firm in Indianapolis.

And he kissed her again as her tears fell when they adopted three children all with different levels of hearing disabilities. And then his kisses were for a rambunctious puppy that seemed to like him best.

He kissed her when they sat hand in hand at their last child's wedding under an arbor covered in bright pink roses. "Still want to kiss me?"

He answered with the gentle press of his lips. "After everything, today, yesterday, and even tomorrow, I promise to kiss you until the day you die. After all, what I've become is because of what I did for you."

"And what I did for you." She smiled and ran her fingers through the gray stubble on his cheek.

For April. For Ryan. For a love hard fought but never ending.

And that was the story of how a robin escaped her cage and finally flew free.

Thank you for reading *For Ryan*. I hope you enjoyed Ryan and April's story. If you did, <u>please leave a review at your purchase site</u>. Reviews are very appreciated by the author. I'm "moose"-assuredly grateful.

Visit www.jillianjacobs.com
for all new release information.

Please enjoy the following excerpt from *Ember's Center,* Book #1 in The O-Line Series. Jillian's Contemporary with Suspenseful Elements.

Owen smiled when she finally met his melted-chocolate eyes.

Seemingly aware she'd given him an once-over—a very blatant once-over. *Awkward.* She clasped together her trembling hands. "Was there something you needed?"

"Yes, actually."

His voice matched his body: deep and heavy, and she bit back a sigh.

"I have a small problem you might help me with."

"Absolutely. What is it?" Ember folded both arms across her chest. *Where are my shoes? Can he see the tea stain on my shirt?*

"I'm glad you agree. You see, I hate when women cry."

What? That was quite the non-sequitur. Laugh lines appeared beside his eyes. Unsure what her answer should be, she replied, "I hate when women cry, too."

Not comfortable around men, especially huge, handsome ones with square jaws sharp enough to cut ice, Ember calmed her breathing and tried stilling her pounding heart. The Marauders' center stood in her cube entry.

Her entry. *Oh no! Where has my mind strayed?*

Did he live up to the rumors? The "O" in Offensive-line raised many a woman's curiosity across social and traditional media platforms since all the players were extraordinarily gorgeous. Not hard to imagine Owen's reputation for bedroom proclivity was very accurate since his shoes were so big, which meant he was big everywhere. *Ridiculous.* She would not stare *there.*

Maintain eye contact. Keep it!

About the Author

In the spring of 2013, Jillian Jacobs changed her career path and became a romance writer. After reading for years, she figured writing a romance would be quick and easy. Nope! With the guidance of the Indiana Romance Writers of America (IRWA) chapter, she's learned many "rules" to writing a proper romance. Being re-schooled was an interesting journey, and she hopes the best trails are yet to be traveled.

Water's Threshold, the first in Jillian's Elementals series, was a finalist in Chicago-North's 2014 Fire and Ice contest in the Women's Fiction category.

Jillian's volunteer efforts include:

- IRWA 2014 and 2015 Program Chair
- IRWA 2015 and 2017 Conference Co-chair
- On The Far Side coordinator for the 2015 and 2016 Fantasy, Futuristic, and Paranormal chapter.

She is the co-founder of Healing with Words—a not for profit agency established for healing survivors of abuse, addiction, trafficking, and prostitution. The mission is to bring together readers, authors, and survivors in a positive manner that affects change and relief from negative influences. Writers on The River, an author event in Peoria, Illinois is hosted by Healing With Words.

Her genres are Paranormal and Contemporary with suspenseful

Connect with Jillian Jacobs:

Website: www.jillianjacobs.com
Twitter: https://twitter.com/GreenMooseProd
Facebook: https://www.facebook.com/GreenMooseProd/
Amazon Author Page: http://bit.ly/JillianJacobsAMZAuthorPage
Goodreads: https://www.goodreads.com/JillianJacobs
Newsletter:
https://landing.mailerlite.com/webforms/landing/q2h3g1

www.ingramcontent.com/pod-product-compliance
Lightning Source LLC
Chambersburg PA
CBHW060439130626
46555CB00005B/2421